HONEYM

By

TIM MYERS

Lighthouse Inn Mystery #8

HONEYMOON FOR MURDER
By Tim Myers

To Patty and Emily.
I wouldn't be writing this one without you both!

Alex and Elise go away to Bear Creek Lodge for their honeymoon, but instead of a relaxing time, they quickly discover that someone died in the room next to them recently. Was it suicide, as the police suspect, or murder, as the newlyweds begin to believe? Their investigation covers the guests at the lodge as well as a new array of eclectic townsfolk, and they soon discover that there is a great deal more going on at Bear Creek than they ever would have suspected.

Chapter 1

It was supposed to be the honeymoon of their dreams.

Instead, it turned out to be a nightmare that Alex and Elise Danton Winston, newly married and very much in love, nearly didn't survive.

"Alex, I can't believe we were lucky enough to get a room at the Bear Creek Lodge on such short notice," Elise Danton Winston told her brand-new husband as they drove closer and closer to the mountain complex where they were about to spend their honeymoon.

"Honestly, luck didn't have much to do with it. Charlie Granger owed me a favor, and I finally decided to cash in on it," Alex told Elise as he patted her knee lightly. Despite what others in Elkton Falls might have thought about Alex's battered old pickup truck, he knew that it would deliver them safely to their destination, and so far, it had done an admirable job getting them to the lodge. "It pays to have friends in high places, doesn't it?" he asked with a chuckle.

"I'll say. I've read about this place online, and it looks magnificent. What exactly did you do for the innkeeper, Alex?" Elise asked. They were currently four hours away from their beloved Hatteras West Lighthouse Inn back in North Carolina, driving deeper and deeper into the Tennessee Mountains toward their goal. When they'd been forced to delay their scheduled honeymoon due to a murder in the family, they had convinced Elise's parents to take the trip instead. The older couple had enjoyed themselves immensely, and they were both now back at their own inn in West Virginia.

"We've known each other for a while now, at least by phone," Alex explained. "Charlie bought Bear Creek Lodge long after I'd been running Hatteras West. Belinda Sheen was his first guest three years ago, as a matter of fact."

Elise smiled at the mention of Belinda's name. "Wow, that woman really loves to travel, doesn't she?"

"Given the limited nature of her chosen territory, she does manage to get around," Alex said with a smile. Belinda had a quirky requirement for traveling, which wasn't all that unusual in and of itself, at least for folks who liked to stay at Hatteras West. The only condition Belinda insisted upon was that her destination had to always be south of the Mason Dixon Line. Alex had asked her about it once, and she'd told him that she had nothing against northerners; she simply couldn't stand the way they drank their tea. If it didn't ooze out of the pitcher due to its high sugar content, Belinda was simply not interested in drinking it, and the woman loved her tea nearly as much as another guest of theirs did, an older man named Evans Graile who stayed with them frequently when he was in the country, even though he lived near the inn.

"So, what does Belinda have to do with how you two got acquainted?" Elise asked him.

"Let's just say that Charlie's opening weekend was less than spectacular. Whatever could go wrong did. His chef quit on opening day, and if that wasn't bad enough, the cook happened to be married to his only maid. They both stormed off in a huff and left him high and dry. Charlie was ready to throw in the towel when Belinda convinced him to call me before he gave up."

"What could you possibly tell him to get him calmed down enough to listen to anything you had to say?" Elise asked him. "Alex, I know how easy you are to talk to, but I can't imagine Charlie being very receptive to a stranger's advice, given the circumstances."

"That's the thing, though. I started telling him about some of my past failures as an innkeeper, all conveyed in humorous form of course, and I had him laughing soon enough. After that, I was able to give him some solid advice, both short term and long, and we became friends, at least via the telephone. The truth is, we've never met, at least not face to face."

"Why ever not?" Elise asked him.

"It's simple enough to answer. We're both innkeepers," Alex said with a smile. As Elise nodded in understanding, he asked her, "When was the last time your parents took a vacation, besides our honeymoon, I mean?"

"I think I was in second grade, but it might have been third," she admitted.

That brought up something he'd been meaning to discuss with her, and this was as good a time as any. "Elise, do you mind that we won't be traveling much once we get back from our honeymoon?" Alex asked her. "I don't have to tell you how demanding Hatteras West can be."

Alex's bride snuggled as close to him as she could manage, given that her seatbelt was still engaged. "Alex Winston, being with you at our lighthouse inn for the rest of my life is all that I want."

Alex smiled at her quickly before looking at the road again. It was too treacherous for him to allow himself to be distracted for more than a single second. This was no interstate they were on now. In fact, it was barely even paved. Charlie's lodge was secluded; there was no doubt about that. But that was what Alex had wanted, a chance to get to know his bride in a brand-new setting without a lot of distraction or interference. When he'd made his request to Charlie for a room, his friend had been delighted to host them. "I'm glad you feel that way, because I do, too," he said.

"The turnoff has got to be coming up soon, doesn't it?" Elise asked as she peered at the map unfolded in her lap. Charlie had warned Alex that GPS was unreliable around the lodge, and it was nearly impossible to get a cell phone signal in the mountains they were in. That was fine with Alex. If there was trouble at Hatteras West while they were away, he didn't want to know about it. There shouldn't be, though, since they hadn't booked any guests, but Emma and her husband, Mor—who also happened to be Alex's best friend—were staying at the inn while they were gone just for good measure.

"It should be around here somewhere. How does anyone ever find him? We get complaints about Hatteras West being isolated, but this is crazy," Alex said, and then he spotted one of the signs they'd been instructed to look for. It was a cut-out piece of plywood twelve inches wide by six inches tall in the shape of a black bear. Within it, there was an arrow pointing to an offcut road just after they had to go over a small, shaky-looking bridge. Alex had to slow down, or he knew that he'd miss the turn altogether.

As they drove the last two miles down what was little more than a beaten path in the woods, Elise said, "Wow, when he said his place was secluded, he really meant it."

"We could always find a hotel in Knoxville or Gatlinburg, if you don't want to spend our honeymoon out here in the sticks," Alex offered. There was nothing wrong with big cities in his mind, but he didn't relish spending his honeymoon amongst crowds of other people. Still, if that was what Elise wanted, he'd do it, with no questions asked.

After frowning for a moment, Elise spoke. "Honestly, places like that are a bit too crowded for me, too, but if you want to go, I'm okay with it," she said tentatively.

Alex laughed for a moment before he spoke again. "Elise, we need to stop tiptoeing around each other. Just because we're married now doesn't mean that things have to change between us."

She joined him in his laughter, and Alex could feel the tension pour out of them both. "I know," she said. "I'm just not sure how to act around you now that we're actually married. I've never had a husband before."

"I've never had a wife, either. Don't change a thing, and we'll be good," Alex said as he suddenly jerked the wheel hard. The left front wheel left the path, and he narrowly avoided hitting a large tree.

"What just happened?" Elise asked after he got them straightened out again and back on the path.

"Did you see that?" Alex asked, his heart rate suddenly elevated well beyond what it should have been.

"See what? What was it, Alex?" she asked. "Honestly, I was looking at you, not the road."

"It all happened so fast I couldn't even say whether it was a man or a woman, but whoever it was came out of nowhere and jumped right in front of the truck," Alex said, slowing down even more and glancing in his rearview mirror to see if he could get a good look at whoever it was that he had almost struck.

"You didn't hit them though, did you? Of course you didn't. We would have felt something. Let's just keep going," Elise said worriedly as she looked up at the sky. Though it was barely past five, darkness was already beginning to creep into the world. The road had been difficult enough to negotiate in the daytime. Alex couldn't imagine how tough it would be traversing it at night. The mountains effectively cut off a great deal of their sunlight, and Alex found himself wishing that someone had built a lighthouse in the mountains there as well. Hatteras West was unique, though, and for very good reason. Building it had been an expensive and massive undertaking, one that his ancestor would never have tackled if it hadn't been for his homesick bride. Alex had often wondered about the enormity of the undertaking when he'd been a bachelor, but now it made perfect sense to him. There was nothing, and he meant absolutely nothing, that he wouldn't do for Elise, including building a tower of her own just for her, if that was what she needed to be happy.

They rounded another bend, and Alex slowed as he passed through two trees that were perched extremely close to the road. He hadn't realized that he'd been holding his breath until they made it safely through.

Finally, they were there at last. As Alex pulled into the gravel parking area, he saw a man standing outside on the porch of the massive lodge. The moment he saw their truck, he grinned and began to wave as he walked toward them. Alex had seen a few pictures on the lodge's website, so he knew that they were being greeted by none other than the owner himself.

Alex got out, and after he held Elise's door for her, he turned to their host. "I'm happy to finally get to meet you," he said as he extended his hand.

"The same goes for me, tripled," Charlie said as he shook it vigorously. He was a slight man, barely over five and a half feet tall, and Alex doubted that he weighed more than a hundred and fifty pounds. He was rugged looking though, with dark-brown hair, a manly bushy beard, and arms that were bristling with muscles. His handshake could have been crippling if he'd wanted it to, but there was nothing but warmth in it for Alex.

After they shook hands, Charlie said, "I can't tell you how happy I am you called, you two." He turned from Alex and offered a hand to Elise. "You must be Elise. I hope you realize how lucky you are having this man in your life."

"As a matter of fact, I'm well aware of it," she said with a smile. "This place is amazing."

Alex glanced at the lodge and nodded in agreement. The building was elegant and yet rustic at the same time. Wooden beams lined the front, and the exterior was made up of weathered gray shingles and large expanses of glass and stone. It looked as though it belonged more on the coast of Maine than buried in the Tennessee mountains.

Charlie nodded with barely a glance back himself. "The original owner grew up on the east coast, and he first built this as a retreat for him and his family before it was converted into a lodge."

"How many rooms do you have?" Elise wondered.

"Eight when we're fully occupied," Charlie replied.

"Is that all? How do you manage to turn a profit?" she asked him curiously.

Alex chuckled. "No shop talk, Elise. We agreed."

"Sorry," she apologized, blushing slightly.

"Are you kidding? I love it," Charlie answered. He might have been small in stature, but there was nothing tiny about his laugh or his smile. He turned to Elise and explained, "The way we do it is we charge premium prices and serve the best food you can imagine."

"Do you have any trouble getting guests?" Alex asked. He couldn't help himself. The innkeeper in him was always searching for ways to make Hatteras West more profitable without making any basic changes in the small-town services he provided for their visitors.

"I know it's remote," Charlie said with a grin. "I took your advice though, and it's really paid off."

Alex frowned. "My advice? What did I say?"

"You told me to find a way to turn all of my negatives into positives. I realized that other lodges were closer to amenities than I was, so I focused on emphasizing the remoteness of the location. The lack of cell phone service was a puzzler at first, but then I realized that in this connected world, there would be people who would pay top dollar for the privilege of being beyond the reach of computer connections and cell phone service."

"There's really a market for that?" Elise asked him.

"You'd be amazed," Charlie said. "Now, let's get your bags so we can get you settled in before dinner. I'm sorry I don't have a honeymoon suite on the premises to offer you."

"Hey, we're just happy you have room for us," Alex said.

His friend's face clouded over for a second before he answered. "Unfortunately, that's not going to be a problem, at least not at the moment."

"Why? What's wrong? Has something happened?" Alex asked him, concerned by his friend's troubled expression.

Charlie started to reply when someone called to them from the road. A large older woman sporting an angry scowl came storming up to them, and she didn't stop until she was inches from Alex's face. She wore tweeds and heavy hiking boots, and she had a hat perched on her head that had seen better days. "Were you trying to kill me back there, you maniac?"

"Helen, take it easy," Charlie said, trying to calm the woman.

"I will not. I was minding my own business when this terror nearly ran me down in his truck, and I demand an explanation," she insisted.

Alex knew how to deal with bullies, which this woman clearly appeared to be. "You're lucky I didn't hit you. Why did you just jump out in front of my truck like that? That's a blind turn in the road, and it's amazing I didn't plow you down. Do you have a death wish or something?"

They held each other's gaze for a few long, tortuous moments, until Helen finally broke the contact, barking out a laugh. "You'd think so after how stupid I just was, wouldn't you?" She slapped Alex on the back. "You know what? You're right. I was wrong. I like you."

"Thanks?" Alex asked, not sure if it was something he should be happy about or not. Her sudden change of attitude had caught him off guard.

"Trust me, it's a good thing," Helen said. "When I'm not being shackled to this place, I run a company with over five hundred employees, and not a one of them has the spine to put me in my place when I need it. How would you like to come to work for me?"

Alex was baffled by this woman's behavior, but he didn't even need to think about her offer. "No, thanks. I already have a job I love."

"We'll be friends, then," she said, sticking out her hand. "I'm Helen Brisbane."

"We're Alex and Elise Winston," he replied, tentatively taking her hand.

After turning to face Elise, Helen studied her for a few moments before asking, "Are you just another pretty face, or is there something lurking beneath the surface?"

Alex didn't even consider speaking up and defending his new wife. Elise was more than capable of doing that herself, and he knew that her good looks were a sore point for her, so it was best that he didn't get involved with that particular exchange. "I suppose you'll have to stop blustering long enough to find out sometime for yourself, if you can ever manage it," she said calmly.

"Woohoo, you're a matched set," Helen said with delight as she clapped her hands together. "Charlie, it's about time we got some fresh blood around here. This place was getting to feel like a ghost town. When's dinner? I'm famished."

"Fifteen minutes," he said, clearly nonplussed by the woman's aggressive behavior.

"What's on the menu? No, don't tell me. I want to be surprised." Before heading inside, she added, "I want to sit with them."

"How long have you been here, Ms. Brisbane?" Elise asked.

"Call me Helen. I was ordered to take a sabbatical from work, and I'm closing in on a month, right, Charlie?"

"Just about," he agreed.

"I've nearly served my time, though. Four more days and then I'm out of here. Well, I'd better go get cleaned up. I'll see you all later. Nice meeting you folks," she said as she rushed into the lodge.

After she was gone, Charlie said, "You'll have to forgive Helen. She's a bit…eccentric."

"That's okay," Alex said with a grin. "We're used to dealing with all kinds of different people. Has she really been here a month?"

"Yes. She had a little incident, and she was told that she either had to disappear for thirty days, or else. At least that's what the board told her. Don't get me wrong. Helen is as sharp as a tack, but as you can see, she has a bit of a temper to go along with it."

Alex found the woman interesting, but there was something else she'd said that had worried him. "What did she mean about it being deserted here, Charlie? Are you in trouble?"

Charlie could only shrug. "Define trouble," he said, trying to brush the question off. "Come on. Let's get you settled in."

"Charlie," Alex said, staying firmly rooted to his spot. Alex wasn't going anywhere until his friend told him what was going on, and he didn't even have to check with Elise to make sure that she didn't mind. After all, her heart was bigger than his.

"Fine. All is not well with my world, but can we talk about it later?" There was a hint of pleading in his voice, and Alex knew that it clearly wasn't the best time in the world to push him.

"Not now, but soon," Alex said. "Promise me that much."

"Okay, I can live with that. Find me after dinner and we'll have ourselves a nice little chat, not that there's anything you can do about it, or even should. You're on your honeymoon, for goodness sakes. You don't need to worry about me and my problems. You're supposed to be making memories."

"That doesn't mean that we can't take the time to help a friend," Elise said.

"You don't even know me, Elise."

"Maybe not, but Alex vouches for you, and that's all that I need to know. If we can help you, we'll do everything in our power," Elise said firmly.

Charlie looked as though he was about to cry, but he managed to bite it back down. "You got yourself a good one, Alex."

"You don't have to tell me," Alex replied. "I'm thankful Elise came into my life every day."

"Let me get your bags," Charlie said as he started for the truck bed.

"If it's all the same to you, we'll carry our own," Elise said. Alex was proud of her, for many reasons, and he knew that Charlie had been right. When it came to spouses, he'd won the lottery, and he knew it. It made it all that much sweeter knowing that Elise felt the exact same way about him.

"I can see that I'm going to have trouble with you two, aren't I?" Charlie asked them with a grin as they carried their own luggage toward the lodge.

"What can I say? Old habits are hard to break," Alex said with a smile. "Lead on."

"Okay, I give up," Charlie answered with a hint of laughter in his voice. "I'm glad you're both here."

"So are we," Alex said as they followed him inside.

Chapter 2

"I hope this will do. You're in number eight," Charlie said as he showed them to one of the guestrooms on the second floor of the lodge. It also happened to be the top floor, where all of the guest accommodations in the building were located. Alex had taken a quick look around as they'd walked into the structure, and he'd taken note of the lobby, the dining room beyond, and what had to be a kitchen just beside that. There were eight rooms on the second floor where they were staying, four on each side, separated by a long hallway. Alex realized that Charlie and his staff must be quartered downstairs, or even off the premises. No, that wasn't likely, as he hadn't spotted any other buildings nearby, and he knew that as an innkeeper, proximity to guests was paramount. There had been a space Alex hadn't seen to the back left of the first floor, and if he had to guess, that was where Charlie and his staff must stay. Alex couldn't help himself trying to fathom the layout of the place. He wasn't entirely sure that it was even a conscious decision to do it; it was just the way his innkeeper's mind worked. Alex was happy that the room they'd been assigned to was on one corner of the building, giving them just one neighbor to share a wall with.

Charlie must have read his mind as he opened the door. "Number seven next door is empty for the foreseeable future, so you should have as much privacy as you ever need."

"How many other guests are staying here at the moment?" Elise asked him.

"Let's see. Val and Carlton Easton are in number one, Helen is in number three, Erica Nance is in number five, and Ian Blackhurst is in number six."

"So, out of eight rooms, four are occupied at your full rate, and one is at a steep discount." Alex hadn't been at all sure about taking the ridiculously low rate Charlie had offered him, but it had been the best he could do, since the innkeeper had been pushing to comp the room for them completely free of charge. "Is it always this bad?"

"No, up until two weeks ago, I didn't have nearly enough rooms for the people who wanted to stay with me."

"What happened two weeks ago?" Elise asked him.

"Like I said, we'll talk about it after dinner," Charlie said as he showed them around. "You've got a king-sized bed, and a nice fireplace, too. The bathtub has a Jacuzzi option, which I highly recommend, especially if you spend any time at all outside hiking. I hope it's okay."

"Okay? It's wonderful," Elise said as she looked around the room with delight.

"You have a great place here, Charlie," Alex said.

"Yes, it's quite nice," the innkeeper said, though he didn't seem all that enthusiastic about it. What was going on? Alex wanted to push him more, but the innkeeper had shut Elise down when she'd probed him, so it was going to have to wait. "Now, dinner will be served soon, so after you get settled in, come on down to the dining room."

He gave them two keys, leaving them on the dresser, and left them alone.

"Alex, he's in real trouble," Elise said the moment their host was gone.

"I know. Don't worry. We'll do everything we can to help. In the meantime, this place really is pretty spectacular, isn't it?"

"It's wonderful," she said. "The truth is that it's even nicer than the first honeymoon we planned."

"Agreed," Alex said. After they put their things away in the dresser and the closet, he turned to his new wife and kissed her. "Wow, I must be slipping. I didn't even carry you across the threshold."

"You only get to do that once," Elise said with a smile as she melted into his arms. "Carrying me across the doorway to the Dual Keepers Quarters was the last time you get to do it, as much as I appreciate the sentiment." She nuzzled his neck for a moment longer, and then she broke free. "I hate to be the one to say it, but we need to go downstairs. I don't know about you, but I'm starving."

"To be continued," Alex said with a grin.

"You betcha," she answered with a lilt in her voice that he absolutely adored.

Charlie was talking with a small group by the time Alex and Elise made their way downstairs. It almost seemed as though the gathered guests were waiting for the newlyweds.

"Sorry if we're holding up the show," Alex said as they joined the group.

"It's not you," Charlie said. "Our chef had a little trouble scheduling today, and if I've learned anything since she's been here, it's that you can't rush Carrie Dale."

"I'm just glad you weren't waiting for us," Elise said.

"Since you're here and we have a few minutes, let me introduce you to your fellow guests. You've already met Helen," he told them. She waved and grinned at them both impishly. "Mr. and Mrs. Winston—Alex and Elise—may I present Val and Carlton Easton?"

"Is there something you find amusing about us, Mr. Winston?" Carlton asked Alex pointedly. He was tall and skinny, and every hair on his head was perfectly in place. Somewhere in his late thirties, Carlton Easton wore a snazzy suit, which had to have been custom tailored to his frame. The only concession he made to being at a resort was that he'd foregone wearing a tie, something that clearly made him uncomfortable.

"Sorry. It's just that no one's ever introduced us as Mr. and Mrs. Winston before, besides the minister," he replied with a sheepish grin.

Val nudged her husband's arm. She was petite, barely an inch over five feet tall unless Alex missed his guess. A pretty brunette, it was obvious that she was quite a bit younger than her husband, and Alex had to wonder if she wasn't the second, or perhaps even the third, incarnation of Mrs. Easton. "They're on their honeymoon, C."

"We are indeed," Elise replied, and to Alex's surprise, she actually blushed a little acknowledging it. It was clear that they were both going to have an adjustment period before they were comfortable admitting that they were newly married.

"How quaint," Carlton said, obviously not caring about their marital status in the slightest.

"You'll have to forgive my husband," Val said. "He doesn't have a romantic bone in his body."

"That's not true," Carlton said primly.

His wife touched his arm lightly and smiled at him. "Of course it's not. I was exaggerating."

"Well, I wish you wouldn't do that," Carlton said, mildly rebuking his wife.

"Yes, dear," she said as she winked at Alex and Elise. Alex wondered how the two of them had ever become a couple, or more importantly, what was keeping them together.

Charlie turned to the other man and woman standing nearby. "And finally, this is Ian Blackhurst and Erica Nance."

"We're not a couple, though," Ian said quickly, as though there was any doubt in the matter. He was tall and muscular, somewhere in his mid-twenties, and Alex had to wonder what line of work he was in. His clothes were more along the lines of what Alex wore, not exactly fit for their surroundings.

"You don't have to sound so happy about it," Erica Nance replied a little testily. The most Alex could say about her was that she was average; in build, in height, in weight, and in appearance. At least until she smiled. When she grinned, though, her entire face lit up, and she was suddenly quite lovely. Alex had never seen anything like it before in his life. The woman's personality seemed to absolutely leak beauty to her exterior. Her clothes seemed simple enough, but he noticed that Elise was studying the woman's attire carefully.

"Is it true? Are you two really newlyweds?"

Alex took his bride's hand in his. "We are. What brings you here, Erica?"

She looked around. "A whim, plain and simple. I wandered in off the beaten path a few weeks ago and decided to stay. Fortunately, Charlie was able to accommodate me."

"You're welcome to stay as long as you like," Charlie said.

"I appreciate that," Erica said without letting herself be distracted. "Tell me, what do you do for a living, Mr. Winston? Pardon my frankness, but I'm a curious kind of gal, so I tend to ask a lot of questions that are none of my business."

"We're both innkeepers," Alex admitted gladly, "and it's not intrusive at all."

She smiled radiantly again as she turned to Ian Blackhurst. "See? Some people don't mind me asking them nosy questions."

Ian muttered to himself, and then he said, "Excuse me."

After he walked away, pretending to study an old map framed and hung on the opposite side of the room, Erica said softly, "He's offended by the slightest question, so I make it a point to ask him as many as I can."

It was clear to Alex that Ian's reaction to the very thought of being paired with Erica hadn't been their first interaction, and it was just as obvious that Erica was taking great delight in tweaking the man every chance she got.

A heavyset woman in her forties approached Charlie, coming directly from what had to be the kitchen. She wore white, from her hat to her shoes, and it was clear that this was their tardy chef. "Sorry for the delay, Charlie, but we're ready now."

"No worries," he said, and then he introduced her to Alex and Elise. "This is Carrie Dale, chef extraordinary, I was telling you about. Carrie, may I present the Winstons, Alex and Elise?"

"These are the newlyweds you were telling me about," the chef said with a smile. "Welcome to Bear Creek Lodge."

"Thanks," Alex said.

After a brief nod, she headed back to the kitchen as Charlie turned to the assembled guests. "Let's eat, shall we?"

As the group made their way to the dining room, Alex saw that there were cozy tables for two set up all around the room. A large sliding glass door opened to a patio dining area, but since it was November in the mountains, it was too cold to eat outside. Along the short side of the room, there was a fireplace with logs burning crisply in it, emitting the nicest warmth and aroma. Alex loved fires, and he and Elise enjoyed them at Hatteras West whenever the temperatures outside took the slightest dip. As soon as Alex saw that folks were seating themselves, he led Elise to a table that allowed them an unobstructed view of the fireplace. Apparently they were going to have themselves a quiet, intimate dinner, which was only fitting, given their status.

To his surprise, though, Helen Brisbane grabbed a chair from a nearby table and pulled it over to where they were sitting. "Mind if I join you?"

Well, Alex had been warned. She'd said that she wanted to eat with them, and evidently the woman usually got what she wanted. He'd been hoping that Helen had been kidding about joining them when they'd first met her, but clearly the woman had meant what she'd said. He was about to protest, in as kind a manner as he could manage, when Elise said, "We'd be delighted."

So much for Alex's polite dissent. It appeared that they would be sharing their table after all.

Charlie noticed though, as any good innkeeper would. He walked over and smiled at them. "Helen, I was wondering if you might join me at my table?"

"Thanks, but I'm eating with them," she said, oblivious to the suggestion.

"Are you sure? I'd really like your company tonight." Clearly he was doing his best to give them a little privacy.

"Then pull up a chair and join us," Helen said. "The more the merrier, right?" she asked the newlyweds.

At that point, there was no sense in turning down the request. After all, what was one more, when three was already a crowd?

"We'd be honored," Alex said. At least the tables were large enough to accommodate four people. They would probably hold ten comfortably, and Alex wondered yet again at the lack of paying guests at the lodge.

Elise chimed in, "Please, do join us."

Evidently it was an offer the innkeeper couldn't refuse. As Charlie made it a foursome, Alex looked around the room. The Eastons, Erica, and Ian occupied the three remaining corners of the room. It was almost as if each of them couldn't get far enough away from their fellow guests, and Alex had to wonder if there was something else going on at Bear Creek that he wasn't aware of. He was still pondering the situation when a young woman wearing a crisp server's uniform came in. She had curly red hair that was clearly difficult to contain, and happy green eyes.

"Good evening," she said as she approached her boss's table first. "May I start you all off with drinks?"

"Sure thing. I'll have sweet tea," Charlie said. "By the way, Zinnia, these are our new guests, Alex and Elise Winston. They're staying in number eight." He turned to Alex and Elise and said, "Zinnia Frost is our chief server and head domestic engineer around here."

She grinned. "There's no need to embellish my titles, Charlie. I'm a waitress and a maid. I'm pleased to meet you both. Now, what would you like to drink?"

"Tea sounds good to me," Alex said.

Elise nodded and then added, "Zinnia is a lovely name."

The waitress grinned, showing her dimples. "My mother is a flower-garden nut. I have three sisters: Rose, Lilly, and Daffodil, though we all call her Daff for short. Okay, sorry about that. That was way too much information. Ms. Brisbane? What would you like?"

"I'll have my usual, but this time, I'd prefer a little more bourbon and a lot less Coke, if you please."

"Yes, ma'am," Zinnia said, and then she moved off to take drink orders from the others.

"How do you manage with one person acting as the waitress and the maid?" Elise asked Charlie.

"We usually have more folks working, but Zinnia was nice enough to pitch in after we got shorthanded." There was more than a hint of trouble in his gaze, but Alex bit his lip to keep himself from discussing it. As promised, there would be time for that later.

After the drinks were delivered, Alex was surprised to find that they weren't given menus. Instead, a few minutes later, plates were conveyed to each place setting. Charlie must have noticed his confusion. "Our chef provides one menu to our guests. It's a little unusual, but it seems to work."

"I think it's brilliant," Helen said, working on her second cocktail already. "That way she only has to worry about prepping one meal for everyone."

"What if someone doesn't like what she's serving?" Elise asked, clearly curious about the quirk.

"Once you taste whatever she decides to make, trust me, you'll like it," Helen said confidently as she finished her drink. As Zinnia placed a plate in front of her, Helen said, "One more, please."

Zinnia looked discreetly at Charlie, who nodded circumspectly. "Of course," Zinnia said smoothly, "as soon as everyone else has been served."

"Of course," Helen said. Alex suspected that she'd seen the exchange between the two staffers, but she chose to ignore it.

Elise was next to be served, and then Alex. He looked at the offerings on his plate, and he nearly started drooling. A small filet mignon was accompanied by asparagus tips, a potato medley, and a bit of some type of cranberry compote. The aromas coming from the plate were almost enough to consume in and of themselves. They were robust and full of flavor, and after Alex took his first bite, he knew that he was in good hands. The food seemed to vanish from his plate, and it was all that he could do to keep himself from asking for seconds.

When he looked up, Charlie was grinning at him. "What do you think?"

"It was amazing," he admitted. "You're lucky to have her."

"I know. I just wish I could convince her to stay," the innkeeper said heavily.

"She's leaving?" Elise asked him.

"I'm afraid she's received an offer I can't even come close to matching," Charlie said reluctantly. "We have her for five more nights, and then she'll be gone for good."

"Greener pashtures, I mean pastures, and all that," Helen said, slurring the word a bit before correcting herself. Her plate was mostly empty, but she'd been more focused on drinking her dinner as opposed to eating it. "If you'll all excuse me, it's been a long day."

Helen had a bit of trouble standing, but Charlie was there to steady her. "I'll be right back," he told them as he helped his guest out of the room.

"What do you make of that?" Alex asked Elise softly now that they were finally alone.

"I'd say that she's pretty well lit, wouldn't you?"

Alex nodded. While they didn't serve liquor at Hatteras West, a few guests had been known to slip in a bottle or two over the years, and he was never happy about dealing with overt drunks. The folks who were discreet about their drinking were fine with Alex, but a man had once thrown an almost-empty bottle of gin off the top of the lighthouse observation platform and in the process had nearly nailed another guest with it. "I'd say so. What's going on around here?" he asked her as he looked around the empty settings.

"I'm not sure, but something's clearly amiss," she replied, and then she frowned momentarily as she glanced behind Alex.

Evidently their host was rejoining them. As Charlie sat back down, he said, "Sorry about that. Sometimes it hits her that way, and I've found that it is best to escort her up to her room immediately when she starts slurring her words." He frowned for a moment before adding, "I know what you must be thinking, but three drinks is not over-serving her. On her best days, she shows no effect."

"And on her worst?" Elise asked.

"Lately, she gets quiet and falls asleep. She says it's the only way she can rest at night, and I tend to believe her," he explained with a shrug. "Besides, I'm in no position to ask her to leave."

Zinnia came back with a tray full of desserts, and as she placed a chocolate torte with raspberry glaze in front of Alex, it was all he could do to keep from digging in before the rest of the table was served.

"What happens to Helen's dessert?" he asked Charlie as he finished his own. Zinnia hadn't placed it at her spot, but surely the chef had prepared enough for everyone.

"Don't you think you've had enough, mister?" Elise asked him with a laugh.

"I just hate that she's going to miss it," Alex said, chuckling himself. She knew him too well. He was already thinking about how good another portion would be.

"Helen never eats dessert," Charlie said. "She says she can't bear it. That was amazing, wasn't it?"

"It truly was," Alex said.

"Would anyone like coffee?" Zinnia asked as she joined them.

"I'd better not, or I'll never get to sleep tonight," Alex said.

Elise turned the offer down as well, and Charlie turned to the waitress/maid and said, "We're good here, Zinnia. If you need us, we'll be out back."

"Isn't it a bit chilly for that?" Alex asked their host.

"You wanted to talk, and it's the only place we won't be disturbed. Erica goes into the lobby and reads after dinner, Ian works on his laptop as far away from her as he can get, while the Eastons always take an evening stroll. Don't worry. There are space heaters on the patio, and another fireplace as well. We'll be toasty, I assure you."

"Let's go, then," Alex said, and the three of them made their way outside.

After Charlie lit the heaters and then started the fire in the hearth, he settled in on a couch opposite the one Alex and Elise had taken.

"You've stalled long enough, my friend," Alex said, prepared to push the point if he had to. "Tell us what's going on."

"The truth is, everything was fine here up until recently."

"What changed?" Alex asked him.

"I found a dead body in one of my rooms," Charlie said, and then he settled in to tell his tale.

Chapter 3

"I know it's unpleasant," Alex said sympathetically, "but it's an innkeeper's plight. Unfortunately, guests die all the time."

"That's the thing, though. It wasn't a guest," Charlie explained.

"Alex, maybe we should just let Charlie tell us at his own pace. We can ask questions when he's finished," Elise suggested.

"I'll try my best, but I'm not making any promises," Alex said, and then he sat back and waited for their host to collect his thoughts. While he was waiting, Alex looked around at the trees surrounding the building, and then he heard some rustling within them. Evidently the birds were roosting for the night, and a gentle November breeze wafted through them. It hadn't exactly been warm since they'd arrived, but the temperature was certainly ten degrees above what he'd been expecting it to be, especially since they were in the mountains. Alex knew that the weather could be extremely unpredictable though, offering warm sunshine one week and snow the next, especially this late in the year. He was pulled from his thoughts when Elise reached over and put her hand over his.

He marveled at how natural it felt, and he was still musing about it when Charlie said, "I'll start at the beginning, if you don't mind."

"Whatever works for you," Alex said, and Elise nodded her encouragement as well.

The innkeeper took a deep breath, and then he began to tell them what had happened to turn his world upside down.

"A few months back, I hired Clint Kidde to do some general painting around the place. It seemed as though something was always in need of a fresh coat of paint, and Clint was usually a good guy to have around. Something happened to him the week before he died, though. He got sullen and started to distance himself from everyone else, and it was rare that I saw him smile."

"Did you ask him what was wrong?" Elise asked. "I know I said we should let you tell this, but I can't seem to be able to do it."

Alex smiled gently at her. "You don't have to apologize for anything. If you hadn't asked him, I would have. Let's just play this thing by ear, okay, and ask if it seems important? Is that all right with you, Charlie?"

"It's fine by me," the innkeeper said. "I asked him a few times, but he never wanted to talk about it, and I didn't want to push him. I brought him lunch the day before he died, and I hung around to chat with him. He was painting the gazebo near the lake, and I thought it would be the perfect chance to get him alone."

"There's a lake?" Elise asked. "I must have missed that on the website."

"Sure. Just take the footpath over there, and it's three hundred yards through the trees. There's a small peninsula, and the gazebo is right in the middle of it."

"What did Clint say when you asked him if anything was wrong?" Alex asked.

Charlie shrugged. "He denied it at first and claimed that all was right with the world. I didn't believe him for one second, but what could I do? I couldn't force him to tell me anything, and I was afraid that if I pushed him too hard, he'd leave Bear Creek and never come back. Some of the locals are like that. I had an uncle who was getting some work done on his house in Key West, and he said the slightest thing would offend his contractor, and the man would disappear for days. Anyway, I was about to give up when Clint said something cryptic to me."

"What did he say?" Elise asked, hanging on every word right along with Alex.

"He said that there was nothing anyone could do for him, and then he corrected himself. 'Well, there's one person,' he said, 'but that's not going to happen. I stepped out of bounds, and now I'm going to have to pay for it. The bad thing is that I knew better, but I did it anyhow. It was a loser's bet, but I still took it.' I didn't get it then, and I don't understand it now, either."

"Was Clint a gambler, by any chance?" Alex asked. "If he bet on the wrong horse and lost, then he might have been desperate to pay his bookie."

"No, Clint wasn't like that. As far as I knew, he didn't even buy a lottery ticket. It was clearly just an expression. I didn't know what to make of it, though. When I pushed him a little harder about it, he wouldn't say another word, so I left him alone." Charlie put his head in his hands and started to weep gently. "I should have pushed him. If he'd only talked to me, maybe I could have helped him."

"How did he die, Charlie?"

"He killed himself," the innkeeper said, the words choking in his throat. "I'm not sure why he used one of my rooms to do it, but that's where I found him a few hours after it must have happened."

"It wasn't in number eight, was it?" Alex asked softly. For the most part he didn't believe in ghosts, or even bad luck, but that still didn't mean that he was eager to spend another minute in a room where someone had just killed himself so recently.

"I would never do that to you, especially on your honeymoon," Charlie said, the reproach thick in his voice. "It was the room next door, number seven."

Alex liked that better, but not by a great deal. "You told us that he killed himself, but you didn't say how he did it," he said.

"The police said that he drank some rat poison I had in the shed out back, and supposedly, he died almost instantly. Ever since it happened, I've had guests canceling on me left and right, and none of the locals will even come out here anymore. I don't know what I'm going to do, and what's worse, there's really nothing that I can do. A man died, tragically taking his own life, and I've been left with trying to pick up the pieces."

"When exactly did this happen?" Alex asked him, hoping for something, anything, that might help his friend. If he could put enough distance between the man's death and the present, a fresh slate of guests might wipe away the memories, or at least the worst of them.

"It was just four nights ago," Charlie admitted.

"Is there any chance that it wasn't suicide?" Elise asked, and Alex nodded in approval at her question. It was the very same thing he'd been about to ask himself, and he was comforted in knowing that the two of them thought alike. In particular, he was happy that Elise wasn't squeamish when it came to investigating death, whether it be murder or suicide.

"Chief Laughlin doesn't think so, and apparently neither did the coroner," Charlie said. "In the end, it was just a tragic ending that happened to have occurred at my lodge. There's another problem, though. You see, if I can't fill my rooms with paying guests, and I mean soon, I could lose the place outright."

"Are you that far behind on your mortgage?" Alex asked. He'd inherited half of his inn from his parents, and he'd bartered everything he'd owned to acquire the other half from his late brother, so at least he'd never had to worry about making payments. If he had, he was certain that he would have lost Hatteras West years before himself.

"I can make this month's mortgage payment, though barely, but next month is out of the question, and the local bank is not at all forgiving. I was late with a payment this past summer by three days, and the loan officer told me that if it happened again, I'd lose everything. He'd been a lot nicer when I'd taken out the loan, but he told me that his boss had nearly fired him for loaning me the money in the first place, so I couldn't exactly blame him for my troubles."

"We'll think of something," Alex said. "What about your current guests? Were they all here when it happened?"

"We were full, except for number seven, but some of the

others have already left. Helen Brisbane's been here nearly a month; the Eastons came ten days ago. Erica Nance has been a guest for about two weeks, and Ian Blackhurst showed up an hour after she checked in. The point is, they were all here when I found the body. I don't know why any of them are still staying, but I'm grateful for what I've got." Charlie looked a bit embarrassed as he admitted, "I owe you both an apology."

"Whatever for?" Elise asked him.

"I should have called and warned you as soon as I found Clint's body, but I just couldn't bring myself to do it."

"Don't beat yourself up about it. We would have come anyway," Alex said, though he wasn't positive that it was true. He could imagine a hundred different scenarios of ways to spend his honeymoon with Elise, but being involved in a suicide wasn't one of them. "You need to let us help you," Alex told him.

"As much as I appreciate the gesture, what could you possibly do?"

"Leave it to us," Elise said with a calm reassurance that Alex admired. "We'll figure something out."

Charlie did his best to smile, given the circumstances. "I don't know what it could be, but it's been a big help just talking about it with a few friendly faces. Thanks for that much, at least." The innkeeper stood and stretched, and then he said, "Tell you what. If I need a reference for the next place I work, can I use you two?"

"It's not going to come to that," Alex said.

"I wish I had your confidence," Charlie said wryly.

Alex stood and patted his friend on the back. "Don't worry. I have enough confidence for both of us."

"Am I interrupting?" Ian Blackhurst asked as he came out onto the patio and joined them.

"No, it's fine. How can I help you, Ian?" Charlie asked.

"This came off in my hand," he said as he held up a doorknob. "It's to my bathroom, and I'd kind of like to be able to use it."

"No worries. I'll have you fixed up in no time," Charlie said, faking his sincerity as he took the knob from his guest.

"We'll catch up later," the innkeeper said as he turned back to Alex and Elise for a moment.

She merely nodded, but Alex put a brief hand on the man's shoulder. "We've got your back, okay? We'll figure something out."

"If you say so," Charlie said softly before turning back to Ian. "Now, let's see if we can get this fixed for you."

After the two men were gone, Alex looked at Elise and saw a glimmer in her gaze. "What are you planning, young lady?" he asked her playfully.

"Me? What makes you think I'm planning anything?" Her act of feigned innocence was cute, and he couldn't keep himself from smiling, and a chuckle or two escaped his lips. "Are you laughing at me, Mr. Winston?" she asked him without the slightest hint of anger.

"I would never dream of doing anything of the sort, Mrs. Winston," he replied with a grin of his own. "The question stands, though. You're coming up with a plan, aren't you? Come on; don't be stingy. Let's hear it."

"Okay, guilty as charged. I was just wondering if we shouldn't send out emails to our current mailing list recommending this place. With our collection of frequent guests, surely some of them would be willing to give Bear Creek a chance."

"As much as I appreciate your kindhearted gesture, can we hold off on doing that for a few days?" Alex asked her.

Elise frowned at him slightly, clearly not understanding why he was being so hesitant. "Alex, I thought you liked Charlie."

"I do," he replied, "but until we get more information, I'm not sure we should put our favorite guests in potential danger, are you?"

She was clearly taken aback by that. "Danger? According to the authorities, the man committed suicide," Elise reminded him. "How could they possibly be in danger from that? Depression isn't catching, you know."

"I understand that. All I'm saying is that I'd like to make sure we know what we're talking about before we start recommending this place to anyone. Let's take a day or two and have a look around ourselves first. Then, if everything checks out, we can send out those emails."

"You don't suspect that there's anything nefarious going on around here, do you?" she asked him softly.

"Elise, maybe I'm being jumpy, or maybe it's just because I've seen more than my share of murders to take anything at face value. Am I being overly paranoid? Probably. That still doesn't mean that we're not right to tread cautiously." He smiled at her gently as he reached his hand out to hers, and as she took it, he helped her stand. "Besides, don't you want to check out the gazebo at the lake?"

The weather had turned suddenly chilly as a strong breeze picked up, and not even the fire of the heaters could warm them. "Absolutely. Just not tonight," she said as her teeth began to chatter. "Let's go inside."

"I agree. Go on in. I'm right behind you."

"Always the gentleman, aren't you?" Elise asked him with a smile.

"Would you be terribly disappointed in your new husband if he admitted that though that might be part of it, he also enjoys the view?"

Elise laughed out loud, and then she shook her head. "You're going to be trouble for me, aren't you?"

"I plan on doing my best, my love," Alex said with a smile, and then the two of them went back inside.

Unfortunately, their playful mood was soon ended.

Evidently, there was a brand-new problem at the Bear Creek Lodge, and there was no way that the newlyweds could avoid becoming embroiled in it.

Chapter 4

"I can't believe you want to stay here!" Val Easton yelled at her husband. "It's so you can be around that little tart, isn't it?"

"What tart?" Carlton asked. "Do you mean her?" he asked loudly as he pointed to Elise.

Alex was about to say something when Elise defended herself instead. "Mr. Easton, you don't know me, but I'll warn you to choose your next words very carefully."

"I didn't mean anything by it," he said, apologizing quickly. Alex could see the fire in his wife's gaze. The man had made the right decision not to tangle with her.

"I'm not talking about her," Val said, and then she pointed at Erica Nance. "I'm talking about her."

To everyone's surprise, Erica started laughing.

Val didn't like that for one second. "What's so funny?"

"It's just that no one's ever called me a tart before," she said. "I think I like it."

"It's not at all amusing. You shouldn't flirt with other women's husbands," Val said intently.

"We were talking about a hiking trail she took yesterday," Carlton protested. "For goodness sakes, Val, get a grip. I'm not cheating on you."

"That's what you said the last time, and it turned out that you were lying. Are you lying to me now, Carlton? Are you?" The poor woman looked as though she were about to burst into tears, going from full-on anger to distress so quickly that it gave Alex whiplash.

"I made a mistake," Carlton said softly, his voice taking on a pleading tone that Alex hadn't been expecting. "It was years ago, and I've apologized a thousand times since it happened. I'm not ever going to do it again, Valerie. I love you."

His wife took all of that in, and then she nodded. "I believe you. I love you, too. Carlton, there's something you need to realize. If you ever cheat on me again, I'll kill myself."

It was wildly inappropriate, given what had just happened at the lodge a few days earlier, but no one chastised the woman for her poor word choice. Val Easton was clearly overwrought, and who could blame her?

"Come on. Let's get you upstairs," Carlton said as he put his arm around his wife, showing, for the first time since Alex and Elise arrived, that there was a tender side to him as well.

"I'm sorry for the dramatics, everyone," Val muttered as her husband escorted her up the steps.

Helen met them as she was coming down, started to say hello, but then clearly thought better of it and made her way down to the rest of the group. "What did I just miss?"

"Apparently I'm a tart," Erica said, "at least according to Mrs. Easton, anyway."

Helen patted her affectionately on the shoulder. "Good for you, dear. I knew you had it in you."

Erica seemed even more delighted by the statement than she had been before. "Me, a tart. Imagine that."

"It's not all that difficult to do," Helen said. "Care for a rematch? I feel like another game of checkers, if you're willing."

"I'm ready for you tonight," Erica said. "Nobody beats Erica Nance six nights in a row at anything."

"We shall see," Helen said as the two women took up opposite sides of the board and laid out the pieces. Alex knew that, contrary to what most people thought, checkers could be every bit as bloodthirsty as chess. It seemed simple enough to learn but surprisingly difficult to master.

Ian and Charlie came down a minute later, and the innkeeper approached them as Ian broke off to observe the game. "Did I just hear someone shouting?"

"Val and Carlton had a difference of opinion," Alex said casually, trying to keep things light.

"Again?"

"Does it happen often?" Elise asked him.

"At least four times since they've been here," he admitted. "Do you ever have guests like that at Hatteras West?"

"You'd better believe it," Alex said. "One week we had the Sunshine Twins visit, and it took everything I had in me not to throw them out."

Charlie smiled a little. "There's got to be more to the story than that. How old were they? Ten? Eleven?"

"Seventy-eight, as a matter of fact," Alex said grimly. "But don't let their advancing years fool you. Burt was three minutes older than Curt, and you'd think it made him king of the high land the way he lorded it over his 'little' brother. They bickered from the moment they got up to the second they fell asleep. It was always a wonder to me how they managed to survive each other."

"How did you handle them?" Charlie asked.

"Alex made them climb the lighthouse steps and argue only when they got to the top," Elise explained with a laugh. "You'd be amazed by how winded it makes someone in good shape climbing all of those stairs, but by the time the twins made it up there the first time, they were both too exhausted to talk, let alone argue."

"Unfortunately, I don't have a lighthouse handy," Charlie said.

"Maybe not, but you've got a gazebo on the lake, and from what you told us earlier, it's a good hike away. The next time they have an argument, tell them that the gazebo is the designated yelling zone for the lodge, and once they are there, they can scream all they want to."

"Even if it's dark out?"

"I don't care if it's snowing, hailing, or fire is falling from the sky," Alex said. "There's a fine line between catering to your guests and letting them spoil everyone else's time."

"You know what? I'm going to try it, if it happens again," Charlie said with a full smile of his own.

"My guess is that it's not a question of if, it's a matter of when," Alex and Elise said in near unison.

"Am I missing an inside joke?" Charlie asked.

"It's just something Alex has a habit of saying from time to time," Elise replied with a laugh.

"Well, I'll keep it in mind. Thanks for the tip. Oh, I almost forgot. Hang on one second." The innkeeper ducked into the dining room, and Alex wondered what he was up to. It was getting late, they'd had a long day, and the evening had stretched out even longer.

To Alex's surprise, Charlie came back out with a bottle of champagne and two glasses.

"You shouldn't have," Elise said as she gladly accepted the offered gift.

"I didn't," Charlie answered with a smile. "Do you know a strong-willed woman named Emma Sturbridge Pendleton?" he asked them.

"She happens to be my best friend," Elise answered with a hearty grin.

"Well, she demanded that I present you with our fourth-best champagne and wish the happy couple my congratulations. I'm curious about something. Why the fourth-best bottle on hand?"

"With Emma, it's impossible to say," Alex replied, smiling, knowing that their friends had remembered them and had tried to make their first evening there special.

"Alex, you do realize that we could never drink this by ourselves, don't you?" Elise asked him.

Alex studied the large bottle for a second before nodding. "Are you thinking what I'm thinking?"

"Let's share," she said, and then she turned to Charlie. "Would you mind getting glasses for everyone?"

"You don't have to do that," Charlie protested.

Evidently Helen had been listening all along. "Pipe down, Charlie. The lady offered us a drink, and I say we don't insult her."

"Okay. I'll be right back," the innkeeper agreed.

Soon enough, everyone present had a glass of champagne. Ian asked, "What about the Eastons? Should we save some for them?"

Helen spoke up before anyone else could. "Let them get their own bubbly. Now, if I may, I'd like to propose a toast. To the happy couple, Alex and Elise. May your troubles be less and your blessings be more. And nothing but happiness come through your door."

After they all drank, Elise said, "I love your toast."

"Oh, it's not mine. I stole it from an old Irishman who had a wicked smile, a fondness for whisky, and enjoyed the occasional pat on the rump."

"Thank you, one and all," Elise said. "Now if you'll excuse us, we've had quite a drive, and it's been a long day."

"It has at that," Alex agreed.

As they neared their room, Alex reached out on impulse and tried the doorknob for number seven. He wasn't at all surprised when he found that it was locked.

"What was that all about?" Elise asked him.

"I don't know. I was just curious, I guess. We've had suicides at Hatteras West, even from the lighthouse tower itself, but it doesn't make it any easier, does it?"

"No, but as you said, it's a part of the innkeeper's life." She smiled at him as they stopped in front of their door. "On a happier note, we're on our honeymoon, and nothing is going to take the joy out of it for me."

"Agreed," he said, getting into the spirit of things. After he unlocked the door, he swept Elise up into his arms again and carried her through the doorway.

"Alex Winston, I told you once was enough. When are you going to stop doing that?" Elise asked him as she giggled, taking any sting out of her protest.

"I don't have any plans on quitting anytime soon," Alex said happily. As he put her down, he added, "Mrs. Winston, may I just say how happy I am to be your husband?"

"Say it as often as you'd like, and know that it goes double for me," she replied.

As they got ready for bed, Elise asked, "What do you think

of our fellow guests here?"

"It's an eclectic lot, isn't it?" Alex replied. "Helen seems to be a law unto herself. What I want to know is how she can afford to spend a month away from work."

"You heard what Charlie said. She didn't have much choice. I keep wondering what incident sparked her banishment. It sounds as though her sabbatical wasn't voluntary, but could it have been court ordered?"

"This place is hardly rehab, or a center for anger management. The real question is how do we find out?" Alex asked.

"I suppose we could ask around, or even do a little digging on the Internet ourselves, if we could get our hands on a computer," Elise conceded. "It might be nice to know who exactly we're sharing a living space with, even if it is only temporary. What about Val and Carlton Easton? That doesn't feel like a happy marriage to me, does it to you?"

"He said it himself. He cheated on her," Alex said, his lips pursed into a frown for a moment. "That doesn't bode well for them."

"Val seems to think it's more of a pattern than an anomaly, based on her reaction downstairs during their fight."

"Just for the record, I was going to come to your defense when it seemed as though Carlton was calling you a tart, but I never got the chance. You were quick out of the gate, weren't you?"

"There are some things I won't tolerate," Elise said, "and one of them is being called a floozy."

"Funny, but Erica seemed to be delighted by it," Alex answered with a grin. "Who would have expected that kind of reaction from her?"

"You know, she's really quite lovely," Elise said. "The clothes she wears might look plain, but they're extremely expensive, and those shoes alone must have cost her a fortune. The woman comes from serious money."

"I don't doubt that Erica is rich, but do you mean that she's lovely in her own way, Elise?"

"No, that's not what I meant at all," his bride said a little sternly.

Alex knew what a delicate topic appearances were to his new wife. To him, and in fact, to most of the rest of the world, Elise was a stunningly beautiful woman, and she'd won a number of beauty contests earlier in her life to back that up, but she was so much more than that, something Alex was very much aware of. "Take it easy. I may be impressed with the package, but it's the gift inside that I fell in love with."

She smiled. "Sorry. Old habits are hard to break. Have you seen Erica when she smiles? It lights up the room. My looks are on the surface. I'm so much more impressed by the inner glow she projects."

"Not that Ian Blackhurst seems to have noticed," Alex replied. "He looked appalled when we assumed that they were together."

"There's more to that man than meets the eye," Elise said softly.

"What do you mean?" Alex hadn't gotten any particular vibes from Ian, but then again, he was beginning to suspect that his wife was a much better judge of character than he was.

"He claims not to be interested in Erica, but if you'll watch him the next time they are in the room together, he can't keep from shooting glances in her direction. I'm not sure if he's interested in her as a girl, but he's certainly paying attention to her as a person."

"I'll have to keep my eyes open," Alex said. "What do you think about the staff, what there is of it?"

"I like Charlie," she said firmly. "But then again, why wouldn't I? He's our kind of people, isn't he?"

"What, a struggling innkeeper?" Alex asked with a laugh.

"Yes, but he also seems to genuinely care about his guests."

"What about Carrie?" Alex asked. "Elise, you know fine food better than I do, so let me ask you a question. Is it

normal for a woman with her culinary abilities to bury herself
in a small lodge in the mountains?"

"That food was fit for a five-star restaurant," Elise said.
"You know something? It never occurred to me to even
wonder about that. You've got a sharp eye, sir."

"What can I say? We complement each other," Alex said,
and then he added with a grin, "By the way, you look very
nice today."

She laughed in spite of the lameness of his joke, which told
Alex yet again that he had chosen wisely in marrying her.
He just hoped that Elise always felt the same way about her
choice.

"And that leaves Zinnia Frost," Elise said. "There's
something about that girl that is infectious. I'd hire her in a
second if she ever decided to leave here."

"I like her, too, but can we really afford to hire anybody
else at Hatteras West?" Before Elise had come along, the
lighthouse inn had barely managed to keep out of the red, but
since she'd gone to work with him, they'd been making a
profit nearly ever since. That was completely and totally due
to Elise's impact, and he was wise enough to know it. If she
made a suggestion, he normally readily adopted it, no
questions asked. Of course, now that she co-owned the
place, he wondered if he'd even be consulted before she
moved forward. "You know, we've never really talked about
how we're going to run the inn now that we're married," he
said softly. "Obviously things have changed, now that you
own half the place."

"Maybe through marriage, but Hatteras West is still all
yours, Alex. It's a part of who you are." She stroked his
cheek lightly. "Dear Alex, are you worried that I'm going to
start making wholesale changes without your blessing now
that we're married?"

"No," he said with a grin. "Okay, maybe a little," he
admitted.

"Well, don't even think about it. I won't insist on a single
change unless you're completely onboard with it, too.

Okay?"

"Okay," he said. "Don't get me wrong, you've done a marvelous job since you came into my life, and I don't want that to change."

"I understand," she said, and then she kissed him soundly. "I didn't include it in my vows, but maybe I should have. I'll never do anything intentionally to make you regret marrying me."

"Nor will I," Alex said, growing more in love with her by the second.

Chapter 5

"What was that?" Alex asked Elise as he sat bolt upright in their bed. He glanced at the clock and saw that it was a little past three a.m.

"What is it?" she asked groggily, coming awake slowly. "Alex, what's wrong?"

"I just heard something next door," Alex replied as he jumped out of bed, grabbed his robe, and slipped into his shoes as he left the room. "I'll be right back."

When he got into the hallway though, it was empty.

The door to the room beside them though, the space where Clint Kidde had committed suicide, was slightly ajar. Something had clearly changed since he'd checked the knob earlier and had found it solidly locked.

Elise joined him before he could investigate further. "What happened, Alex? Did you do that?" she asked as she pointed to the cracked door.

"No, that's the way I found it. I'm going to check it out right now," Alex said.

"Here. Take this," Elise said as she handed him the fireplace poker from their room.

"How did you know I might need to defend myself?" he asked her softly.

"When your husband jumps out of bed in the middle of the night, a weapon is probably going to be in order," she said simply.

"Good thinking," he answered. "Are you staying out here, or are you coming with me?"

"There's no way I'm letting you go in there alone. Go on. I'm right behind you," she said.

Alex nodded, and then as he slowly opened the door, he reached in and flipped on the light. The space was empty, but someone had clearly trashed the place, and recently too, unless Alex missed his guess. The bed had been pulled off its frame, and the sheets were awry. Every drawer had been pulled out, and a lamp lay shattered on the hardwood floor. That was the sound Alex must have heard that had awakened him.

"Check the bathroom," Elise said softly, but Alex shook his head as he pointed to the closet first.

"Stand back," he whispered, and then he threw that door open.

It was empty, except for a handful of coat hangers and a few dust bunnies in one corner.

"One last space to check," Alex said in a near whisper as he approached the bathroom. The door was standing wide open, and as he walked into the space, he had the most uncomfortable feeling in the bottom of his stomach that someone was lurking just inside. Flipping on the light, he used the poker to move the curtain back from the shower, but no one was there.

The place was empty.

"What's going on in here?" Alex heard Charlie ask them from the other room. "Alex, why did you trash the place?"

Alex rejoined his wife to find Charlie staring at them with a frown on his face. "We didn't do this," he insisted. "I heard something crash onto the floor over here a minute ago, so I came over to investigate. We must have just missed whoever it was."

Charlie sighed and slumped down a little. "I can't believe this is happening. I can just hear the stories now. Folks in town will be claiming that number seven is haunted, and I'll never get anyone out here to ever help me again."

"This wasn't the work of a ghost, and you know it," Alex said. "Someone was clearly searching for something."

"But what could it be?" Charlie asked. "There's nothing of value here, so why go to all of this trouble?"

"I don't know," Alex admitted as Helen appeared in the doorway.

"I thought I heard voices," she said as she looked around

the room with pure dread on her face. Her complexion was ashen, and she wouldn't put a single foot into the room, clearly preferring to stay out in the hallway instead. "This place is a disaster!"

"We didn't do it," Alex said. "What woke you, the lamp falling?"

"No. I heard voices in the hallway, so I thought I'd investigate. It appears that the rest of the guests here are sound sleepers," Helen added as she looked up and down the empty hallway. "I envy them."

"Well, there's nothing to see here," Charlie said as he tried to lead Alex and Elise back out into the hallway. Before he did though, he asked, "Is there any way that I can convince the three of you not to tell anyone else what you just saw here tonight?"

"I don't know what you're talking about," Helen said as she averted her gaze. "I didn't see a thing. As a matter of fact, I'm not even here," she added. "Good night, all."

"I knew there was a reason I liked her," Charlie said after she was gone. "Why don't you two follow her lead and go back to bed yourselves?"

"Nonsense," Elise said. "We'll hang around and help you make this right again in no time."

"Really, you don't have to do that," Charlie said.

"We'd be glad to. Right, Alex?"

Alex hesitated, though it wasn't because he was afraid of doing a bit of work, even on his honeymoon. The innkeeper in him was too strong not to pitch in and make things right again if he could help. "I'm just wondering about something else. Should we call the police and report the break-in? Maybe we shouldn't touch anything until they get here."

Charlie shook his head. "There's really no reason to even bother. Nothing was taken, and only an old lamp was broken. It was probably just some drunk local visiting the room where Clint died on a bar bet. I don't know how they got through the front door, though. I need to check that out."

"Let's go see," Alex said. "After we check the locks, then

we can decide what to do about the police." Alex had to wonder if there was something a great deal more sinister going on than a simple prank, but ultimately, it wasn't his inn, so the decision whether or not to call the police was Charlie's and Charlie's alone.

The locks downstairs appeared to be fine. "I must have slipped up and forgotten to lock up tonight," Charlie said.

"Don't worry. It happens to me, too," Alex said. "That's the trouble with having guests coming in all hours of the day and night. It makes security rather difficult at times, doesn't it?"

"Tell me about it," Charlie said. "I know big hotels never lock their doors, but I can't afford to do that here. I appreciate your advice on calling the police, but honestly, after Clint's suicide, there's some resentment in town toward me and this lodge, and I'd rather not get them involved, if it's all the same to you."

"It's fine by me," Alex said, though he wondered about the wisdom of the decision.

"That's settled, then. Now, let's go clean that room," Elise said, sounding more chipper than she had any right to, given the time of night.

"You really don't have to help," Charlie added lamely as the three of them all walked back upstairs together.

"Are you kidding? It will be fun," she said.

Charlie shrugged, and then he looked at Alex apologetically. "Sorry."

"Don't be. You heard the lady. Let's knock this out. Between the three of us, we'll be done in no time."

After the room was made right again and the remnants of the lamp were removed, Charlie said, "Sorry for the excitement."

"Unless you trashed the room yourself, there's no need to apologize," Alex replied.

Did the innkeeper flinch at the suggestion that he might have torn the room up himself? Alex couldn't be sure. Maybe it had been his imagination, or perhaps it was just because he was sleepy, which was perfectly understandable, given the time of night and the circumstances.

"Good night, and thanks again for your help," Charlie said, and Alex and Elise disappeared back into their room.

"That was odd," Alex said once their door was shut and locked. To be on the safe side, he flipped a chair backward and placed it under the knob, forming a barrier to entry that was just another level of precaution.

"What's odd?" Elise asked him.

"Did you see Charlie flinch for an instant when I suggested that he may have trashed the room himself?"

"No, I missed that," Elise replied. "Do you think that's really what happened?"

"No, it was probably just my imagination, but there is something I'm wondering about, Elise."

"What's that?"

"How did he get upstairs so quickly? Helen was across the hall, and it took her a few minutes to show up. Charlie sleeps downstairs, and number seven is on the opposite side of the building, so it's not like he heard the noises from below."

"Maybe he was up doing the books," Elise suggested. "We're right over the lobby. In fact, our fireplace flue has to be a part of the one just below it. That would put number seven directly above his desk."

"You're probably right," Alex said as he fought off a yawn. "I'm not sure I'm going to be able to get back to sleep. How about you?"

"I'll be out in thirty seconds, given the chance," she said smugly, "but I'll stay awake with you if you want me to."

"No, we both need our rest. Good night, Mrs. Winston."

"Good night, Mr. Winston," she answered, and much to Alex's surprise, he somehow managed to fall asleep without much fuss himself.

"Good morning," Alex said to Zinnia as he and Elise entered the dining room bright and early the next day. "Are we too early for breakfast?"

"No, we love early risers around here," the redhead said cheerfully. "Sit wherever you'd like, and I'll be right with you."

They chose the same spot where they'd eaten dinner the night before, and Zinnia followed them with two menus. "Breakfast is simple fare, at least compared to the dinners around here," she explained.

"Where do lunches fall in the scale?" Elise asked her with a grin.

"That's usually the plainest meal of the day. Most of the folks who stay with us like to either hike the property or explore some of the nearby towns. There are lots of antique places around, so if you'd like some inside information, I'm your gal. Don't get me wrong. Carrie will be more than happy to feed you, but if it were me, I'd take a field trip and see what I could find out."

"You seem to do a great deal around here," Elise observed.

"Well, I couldn't just abandon Charlie like Sasha and Billie did," she said with a frown. "As soon as Charlie found Clint's body, they both refused to come back to work here."

"And yet you weren't afraid to come back," Alex said.

She shrugged as she said, "It's unfortunate, but sometimes these things happen. It's certainly no reason to quit your job." Zinnia's frown vanished as she plastered a smile back onto her face. "As I said, the menu is a bit limited in the morning, but the oatmeal is out of this world, and the western omelet is superb, too."

"Which would you recommend?" Alex asked her, liking the young woman even more for her loyalty to her employer, despite the trying times. In Alex's mind, fealty was an extremely important quality, and one that he cherished above nearly all else. He flashed back to the time when Elise had first come to the Hatteras West Lighthouse Inn, due entirely to the fact that her cousin, Marisa, had panicked at the first hint of a dead body on the premises and had run screaming from the inn, practically literally.

"I had her whip me up a little bit of both this morning,"

Zinnia said with a grin.

"That sounds good to me then," Alex said as he handed the menu back to her.

"Alex Winston, are you seriously going to have two breakfasts this morning?" Elise asked him with a grin.

"No, I'm simply having two halves that make a whole. Tell you what. You get the same thing, and we'll split them. Come on, Elise. Let's live a little. This isn't just our honeymoon, it's a vacation away from the inn as well, so why shouldn't we enjoy ourselves?"

Elise nodded happily. "Why not? Zinnia, we'll have two orange juices, and ice waters too, if you don't mind."

"It's my pleasure," she said. Their server didn't budge after taking the order, though. "Is it true you two own a lighthouse in the mountains?"

"It's too good to make up," Alex conceded with a grin.

"You don't have any pictures of it, do you?"

Alex was fairly new to the smartphone concept, and his photos still came out looking as though they'd been taken by a kindergartener, but Elise saved the day yet again.

"Here's one of the lighthouse in a snowstorm we had last year," she said as she brought out her phone. The pride in her retelling of the story was enough to warm Alex's heart. His bride truly did love Hatteras West every bit as much as he did. "And here's one taken from the observation deck at the very top," she said, flipping through photos and narrating each one in turn.

"I'd love to see it someday," Zinnia said wistfully.

"You really should. In fact, you're welcome anytime," Elise said.

"I appreciate the offer, but I'm pretty sure that I could never afford to stay there."

"Tell you what. We'll give you the friends and family discount," Alex said. Anyone who showed any interest at all in his lighthouse was almost an automatic friend for him.

"Be careful what you offer. I might just take you up on that," she said.

"We hope that you do," Elise replied as Charlie walked in, spotted them, and then headed toward their table.

Alex noticed the way Zinnia looked at him, and he wondered if she wasn't smitten with her boss, at least a little. He'd have to ask Elise later. She was usually much better about picking up on those clues than he was.

"Coffee and some oatmeal, please, Zinnia," Charlie said distractedly. "May I join you two?" he asked as he glanced at Alex and Elise.

They both nodded, and Charlie took a seat.

Zinnia still hadn't moved from her spot, though.

"Is there something I can do for you?" the innkeeper asked her briskly.

Zinnia didn't miss a beat. "Good morning. I slept great, thanks for asking. Yes, it is indeed turning out to be a beautiful day, though we're supposed to get a great deal more rain later, at least according to the forecast I heard earlier on the radio."

Charlie stared at her for a second, and then he shook his head, looking instantly remorseful. "Forgive me. I was up most of the night trying to make sense of my books, among other things." He glanced at Alex and Elise as he added the last bit, hiding the fact that they'd been cleaning up a trashed guestroom not that long ago. "How are you, Zinnia?"

"Honestly? I'm embarrassed," Zinnia said. Being a redhead, she had the loveliest blush, and it reminded Alex of Erin Murphy, a girl he'd dated in high school. She'd had the prettiest red hair, the palest skin, and the cutest freckles he'd ever seen, though she'd been extremely self-conscious about all three. "I'm sorry for picking at you, boss."

"Nonsense. You had every right to put me in my place," Charlie said.

After she was gone, Elise looked at Charlie for a second, and then she said, "You really should be nice to that poor girl."

"I know. When everyone else abandoned me, Zinnia stayed on. She's a real treasure, and I know I don't tell her that enough."

"Sure, that's reason enough," Elise explained, "but she also happens to have a major crush on you."

Charlie looked startled by the news. "Zinnia? A crush? I highly doubt it."

"Alex?" Elise asked him for confirmation.

"Even I saw it," Alex admitted, "and if that's the case, it's got to be hard to miss. Hey, don't just write her off. Elise started out working with me, and look how that ended up."

"Even if it were true, which I highly doubt, I have too many troubles to deal with romance in my life right now."

"I'm just saying," Elise replied. "Sometimes you don't have a great deal to say about it."

"Maybe, but with everything I have on my mind right now, it's not going to happen, period. Every time I turn around, something else seems to happen."

Chapter 6

"Are you talking about the break-in last night?" Alex asked him softly.

"No, something else has come up since then," Charlie answered as Zinnia came back with their drinks.

Charlie must have been staring at her, perhaps wondering if what Alex and Elise had said had been true, because the waitress/maid noticed the extra attention. "Is there something on my face?" she asked as she wiped a phantom smudge away.

"No, it's nothing like that," Charlie said.

"Then what is it? Boss, you're looking at me funny."

Charlie was the one who appeared to be embarrassed by her comment. "Sorry. I was just lost in my thoughts for a second there."

"Okay then," Zinnia said, though it was obvious that she didn't believe it for one second. She glanced at Elise, not Alex, for confirmation, but Elise simply shrugged. Zinnia shrugged back in response, and Alex had to wonder just how much information had just been shared in that particular wordless conversation.

"Now, tell us about your problem this morning," Alex said after taking a sip of water.

"I shouldn't keep burdening you with my woes," Charlie said. "You two are on your honeymoon, for goodness sake. You don't need to hear my troubles."

Elise answered for Alex, something he heartily approved of. "Charlie, the three of us are part of a loyal order that goes back for centuries. Being an innkeeper is a taxing yet noble profession, and if anyone can understand what you're dealing with, it's the two of us. If we can ease your load in any way, not only do we consider it our obligation, but it is a privilege to be able to step in and help."

"Is she always prone to making speeches like that?" Charlie

asked Alex with a smile.

"She doesn't make them nearly enough, if you ask me," Alex replied. "Elise takes our profession seriously, and so do I. Enough excuses, sir. What can we do?"

"If you really mean it, I've got an order of supplies in town that they refuse to deliver. If I don't get them in the next three hours, we'll all be eating peanut butter and jelly sandwiches for dinner. I'd go myself, but Helen asked me last week to set some time aside this morning for her, and I'm in a real bind."

"We'll be happy to go," Elise said. "Will our truck hold everything, or do we need something bigger?"

Alex loved the fact that his bride enjoyed his beat-up old pickup as much as he did. She'd even driven it a time or two, but mostly he liked being behind the wheel.

"No, everything will fit nicely in your truck bed," Charlie said. He pulled an invoice out of his pocket and said, "Here's the master list. If you don't mind, check everything off as you load it. Sandy Hearns has been known to short me occasionally and then feign ignorance when I call him on it. I appreciate this more than I can say."

"Don't think another thing about it," Alex said as he took the list and put it in his flannel shirt pocket. "As soon as we finish eating, we'll head into town. What's the name of the place we're going?"

"Star Ridge Mercantile," he said.

"I'm curious about something," Elise asked him. "How did the town get its name? Is there a ridge where you can see the stars particularly easily?"

"As a matter of fact, there is. It makes for a nice hike, but to be honest with you, I like to go to the lake and look at them from the gazebo at night. They're really beautiful. Even folks from town come out and stargaze there."

"It's nice that you let them do that," Alex said. "We have a formation near the lighthouse called Bear Rocks, and we let people from town explore them as well."

"And don't forget the lighthouse itself," Elise said. "Alex

is much too modest. He opens the lighthouse to the residents of Elkton Falls. There's even a group called the Stairsteppers that have recently started meeting and using the climb for exercise."

"They meet three times a week before most folks are even awake, so it's really no bother," Alex explained.

"Still, it's good of you to do it," Charlie said. "Aren't you worried about your insurance though? I've been concerned that someone might fall off the gazebo and into the lake. I could lose my resort if that happens, couldn't I?"

"We carry extra insurance for things like that," Alex admitted, "but fortunately, we don't have to pay for it."

"How did you manage that?" Charlie asked, clearly interested.

"One of our guests covers it. The man's father was murdered at the top of the lighthouse, and Elise and I solved the case. Junior was so thankful that he covers the policy for us every year."

"Unfortunately, I don't have any guests quite that loyal to me. How did the man happen to die?" Charlie asked.

Just then, their breakfasts arrived. Alex had been wondering how they were going to split their orders, but clearly Zinnia had already told Carrie, who had provided separate bowls and plates for their meals.

"Let's say we table that story for another time," Elise suggested. "Right now, let's just enjoy our breakfasts."

"Agreed," the innkeeper said, and then he turned to their waitress as she put his oatmeal in front of him. "Thanks, Zinnia. I know I don't say it enough, but I really do appreciate you sticking around, and for all of the things you do for me at Bear Creek."

"Of course," she said, blushing again. "Can I get you anything else?"

Alex surveyed the offering and smiled. "I think we're good. Thanks."

"You're welcome," she said, still blushing as Val and Carlton Easton walked into the dining room. They gave the table a pair of curt nods before taking up their former spot as well, which was conveniently as far as they could get from the others.

"Have you noticed how quickly people become creatures of habit?" Elise asked after taking a bite of oatmeal and smiling. "How did you know that I had the same thing for breakfast every morning? You just got here," Charlie said.

"I'm not talking about the food. We sat right here at this table last night, and the Eastons were right where they are now. I'm willing to bet that the others take the same spots as well."

"You'd be right about Ian and Erica, but Helen never eats breakfast." Charlie glanced at his watch as he added, "In fact, she should be back from her walk shortly. She'd better be. We have to meet soon."

"What did she do to get banished here?" Alex asked their host, no longer able to contain his curiosity.

"I'm sorry. I know you're both helping me out a great deal, but I don't feel comfortable talking about one of my guests. Feel free to ask her yourself, but it's not my story to tell. I hope you understand."

"Of course we do," Elise said smoothly, though Alex suspected that she wanted to know the answer to that question at least as much as he did. "How did you happen to lure Carrie out here to the lodge? With her skills, I'd think that she could work anywhere in the world." Elise must have realized how that sounded, because she quickly added, "Not that this place isn't wonderful in its own right."

"You don't have to sugarcoat it for me," Charlie said. "I know how lucky I am to have her. Carrie is from around here originally, and when she moved back home to be closer to her aging mother, I snapped her up before anyone else could. I'm not foolish enough to think that she'll be here forever, but I'll take her as long as I can have her. I haven't given up on talking her into extending her stay here with me. She's really something, isn't she?"

"She is indeed. I wonder what she does to this oatmeal to

make it so special?" Elise asked after eating another bite.

"When you finish, you should go back and ask her," Charlie urged her. "Alex has told me countless times how good you are in the kitchen yourself."

Alex nodded. "It's no secret."

Elise simply shrugged. "I'm good enough to get the job done on my best days, but this is an entirely different level. Do you think she'd mind if I asked? Some chefs are extremely protective about their dishes."

"I honestly believe that she'd love the company. I imagine it's kind of lonely in the kitchen these days."

"I'll do just that, then," she said. "I'm nearly finished, anyway. Gentlemen, would you excuse me?"

"Absolutely," Charlie said, and Alex nodded his agreement as well.

After she was gone, Alex turned to the innkeeper and asked, "Have you thought any more about what happened last night?"

"The break-in? No, not really," the innkeeper admitted.

Alex wasn't buying it, though. "Come on. This might be the first time we've actually met, but we've been friends for years. I can tell when you're holding out on me."

"Of course it's bugging me," Charlie admitted in a soft enough tone to keep the Eastons from hearing him. "I've been wracking my brain trying to come up with a reason besides a prank that anyone would want to trash that room."

"It has to be connected to Clint Kidde's death, doesn't it?" Alex asked.

"What did they expect to find? The police might not have given the place a thorough search, but from what I was told, it was pretty cut and dried. They found some kind of drink bottle full of rat poison near the body."

"How about the original container? Was that in the room as well?"

"No," Charlie responded with a frown. "Why, should that matter?"

"I don't know," Alex admitted. "It might, though."

"Listen, I've heard the rumors about you investigating murders around your inn in the past, but this was suicide, plain and simple." Charlie seemed almost defiant in his statement, as though he were daring Alex to dispute it.

"I'm not saying that it wasn't," Alex amended, trying to take the sting out of his next statement. "It just seems odd to me that the man would kill himself in one of your rooms if the poison was in an outbuilding and he was working on the gazebo down by the lake. Surely the police wondered about that as well."

"I don't have a clue why he decided to kill himself there, nor do I know what the police think. If they suspect anything sinister, they haven't said anything to me. Maybe you should ask them yourself."

Why was Charlie suddenly being so defensive? "Hey, I'm on your side, remember?" Alex asked, trying to add a smile to ease the bluntness of his reminder.

"I know," Charlie said, the steam seeming to leave him abruptly. "I'm barking at everyone in sight, aren't I? How did you handle running the inn all that time before Elise showed up on the scene?"

"I did the best I could, and that was all that anyone should expect of themselves." Alex put a hand on his friend's shoulder. "You're doing okay, my friend."

"I don't know. I certainly try, but there are times when I'm not sure that it's enough, you know?"

"Hey, if you didn't have doubts every now and then about your chosen profession, you wouldn't be human. Did I tell you about the time I had a toddler flush his toys down every toilet in the inn? It was a nightmare, and when I told the parents about it, they just shrugged it off, saying that boys would be boys, so what could they do? To make matters worse, they tried to skip out altogether the moment I turned in for the night."

"What did you do?" Charlie asked, clearly happy to have a distraction from his own woes.

"Fortunately, I had an imprint of their credit card, so they paid for my plumbing repairs as well as their stay. They must have forgotten that I'd taken it when they'd first checked in. You should have heard them howl when they got their bill a month later."

"Weren't you afraid of losing their business, Alex?"

"Afraid? Just the opposite. I was counting on it! I would have banished them forever myself, but Elise talked me out of threatening them. We never heard another word from them, which was fine with me. It's funny, but over the years, I've found that twenty percent of my guests cause eighty percent of my headaches. Most folks are a joy to host at the inn. If I could only figure out a way to winnow that twenty percent down by even a few percentage points, I'd be a happy man."

"What are you two talking about?" Elise asked as she rejoined them. "Alex, are you telling Charlie some of your tales of woe again?"

"I don't mind. In fact, I like hearing them. I find them comforting, for some reason," the innkeeper said with the first smile Alex had witnessed in a while.

"I was telling him about Toilet Boy," Alex said with a grin.

"Ah, the Scarlet Flusher," Elise said with a nod. She turned to Charlie. "Wow, Carrie is a real treasure. You'll never believe what the secret ingredient to her oatmeal is."

"What is it?" the innkeeper asked, catching a bit of Elise's enthusiasm.

"Sorry. I've been sworn to secrecy. If you want to know, you'll have to ask the chef herself," Elise said with a laugh. "You're not the only one who respects other people's right to their secrets."

"Touché," he said.

Elise turned to Alex. "Are you ready to head into town?"

"I am," he agreed as he stood. "Is there anything else we can do for you while we're gone?"

"This is more than enough," Charlie said. "Don't worry about paying. I have a tab at the Mercantile."

"Then we're off," Alex said.

It was still cold out, so after grabbing their jackets, Alex and Elise let the truck warm up a little before driving off. As they sat there, they saw Helen Brisbane walk past them, oblivious to their presence. Evidently she didn't realize they were even there, because she was dabbing at her cheeks not from the cold but from chasing tears tracking down.

The woman had clearly been crying, and Alex and Elise were suddenly determined to find out the reason why.

Chapter 7

"Helen? Are you okay?" Elise asked their fellow guest as she and Alex got out of the truck.

Helen Brisbane looked startled to see them there, and she did her best to make a hasty escape.

Alex wasn't going to let that happen, though.

"I know we just met, but you should consider us friends. Did something happen on your hike?" he asked her.

"No, I'm fine," she said, though it was clear that she was not.

"You don't have to tell us if you don't want to," Elise said sympathetically, "but you should at least tell someone. You'll feel better if you do."

"I'm dealing with it. Seeing that room again last night brought back some unpleasant memories," she admitted softly. "Just when I think I've got a handle on it, I fall apart again."

"That's right. Charlie said that you were close by when he found the body," Alex prompted her. "Had you had any contact with the victim before he died?"

"'Victim.' How I hate that word," Helen said. "I heard Charlie shout when he found…Clint. Naturally I opened my door to see what was going on. How I wish that I hadn't! The sight of him lying there on the floor will haunt me until the day I die."

"Maybe it's time you moved on to someplace where you aren't reminded of what happened," Alex said. He hated driving off one of the most reliable guests Charlie had, but then again, why should this woman keep torturing herself with the memory of seeing the dead painter's body?

"That's just it. I can't. I'm not allowed to," she said. This was not the bold, brash woman Alex had already grown accustomed to seeing. This Helen was timid at the moment, and though he would have said it was nearly impossible before he'd seen her like she was, she actually seemed afraid, weak, and broken.

"Why can't you leave?" Elise asked her gently. "What happened that brought you to Bear Creek Lodge in the first place? I can't imagine being banished for a month from the business you run. It sounds like cruel and unusual punishment to me. How bad could your actions have been?"

It was a bold, direct inquiry that didn't seem that way at all to Alex. Elise had asked it so that the question was full of caring, not just a tactless probing for information.

"I punched one of my board members on the nose."

"What made you do something so radical?" Alex asked her.

"He suggested that I was no longer a viable option to run the company I created. The man insisted that I should step aside and let someone younger, more capable take over. He told me in front of the entire board that I was over the hill, frail, a weak and ineffectual leader. I blew my stack, and the next thing I knew, I was showing him that I wasn't the frail old woman he claimed I was. I regret that I let him goad me into physical violence. What I should have done was bided my time and eased him out," she admitted. "Once I hit him, though, there was no going back. I faced three unequally appetizing choices: take a month off; attend anger management classes for a year; or face arrest. Of the three choices, I figured this was the least onerous. After what happened to Clint though, I'm not so sure that I was right."

So, Helen Brisbane had verified occasions of fits of temper and acting rashly and on impulse. In a way, it didn't surprise Alex all that much. The woman clearly had a dramatic flair, and she seemed to take joy in pushing people a little to test their limits. Had she given the painter a nudge as well, perhaps, taunting him about something he was already sensitive about? If she had, the suicide had probably come as a surprise to her, a deadly and crushing bombshell. "I asked you something earlier, but I don't believe you ever answered me. Did you know Clint Kidde?"

Helen looked at Alex as though he was the bully, and then suddenly, she fled from them, racing inside as if getting away from him was the only thing that mattered.

"What just happened? Did I say something all that wrong?" Alex asked his wife. "I just wanted to know what kind of contact she had with the man who died."

"It was a legitimate question," Elise said, "But Helen seems to be right on the edge of holding it together, so it didn't take much to push her over. I wonder if we should go after her."

"I don't know how I could make things any better at this point, and I'm not at all sure that I wouldn't make them worse," Alex said. "When we get back, I'll apologize to her then. Maybe if she has a little time to reflect, she'll realize that I didn't mean to upset her."

"Dear, sweet, Alex, apologizing without even truly knowing why," Elise said. "You're a noble soul, aren't you?"

"I'd hope that if our roles were reversed, someone else would do the same for me," he explained. "It's simple common courtesy."

"Unfortunately, it's not all that common anymore."

"Well, it should be, at least if you ask me," he said.

"And that's what makes you so loveable. Now come on. Let's go into town and get that order for Charlie."

"That sounds good to me," Alex said. The conversation with Helen had left him unsatisfied, both in the answers he'd gotten and with the woman's reactions to his questions. Why was she so sensitive about his questions? Alex knew firsthand how unsettling a dead body could be, but it still didn't explain her reaction. He was glad they had an errand in town to run. A change of scenery would be most welcome. Alex tossed his wife the truck keys, and she deftly picked them out of the air. "Why don't you drive?"

To his surprise, Elise threw them right back to him. "Thanks, but I believe I'll pass. I'll drive it around town if you want me to, but I saw the road we came in on yesterday. There's no way I'm going to take a chance of scratching your truck."

Alex laughed. "It would be fine if you did. After all, how would anyone even be able to tell?" he asked as he patted the door lightly.

"You'd know it, and so would I," she said, "and in the end, that's all I care about. Now, let's go get those supplies. I can't wait to see what Carrie has in store for us tonight."

The mercantile was laid out completely differently from Shantara's place back in Elkton Falls, with food playing a predominant role in the space. There were still plenty of hardware supplies and touristy items available for sale—including postcards, shot glasses, and T-shirts—but food was clearly king there. Alex looked around, wondering how the merchant managed to keep up with fresh food as well as their other offerings. For him, it would be a complete and total nightmare. On the other hand, some folks might have found his job rather daunting, since owning and working at an inn took a great deal of repetitive labor, but it was something Alex loved doing. Besides, if he ever needed a break, all he had to do was step outside and look up at the lighthouse. It always managed to revive his spirits, even in the worst of times.

"May I help you?" a young woman asked as she approached Alex and Elise. He saw that her nametag said that her name was Cindy, and Alex was a big fan of using people's names when he spoke with them. She greeted them with a broad smile and seemed eager to assist them in any way that she could.

"Hi, Cindy. We're here from the Bear Creek Lodge," Alex said, pulling the invoice from his pocket. "We understand you have an order for us that we need to pick up."

The temperature suddenly got very icy inside. "Oh. Sure. Wait right here."

It was an order, not a request, and Alex looked at Elise once the woman was gone. "Was it something I said?" he asked her. "She seemed really nice when we first came in."

"It wasn't you, but it does seem to be a bit frosty in here all of a sudden, doesn't it?" Elise asked.

"They really don't seem to like Charlie, do they?" Alex asked.

"I'm not sure what's going on, but for some reason, they aren't real fans."

"You shouldn't be here," an older man with dirty-blond hair said sternly as he approached them.

"Excuse me? Have we done something wrong? First Cindy gives us grief, and now you're telling us that we don't belong here. Is that the way you treat all of your customers?" Alex asked with a slight smile and a sense of genuine curiosity. He wasn't about to put up with such overt insolence, but that didn't mean he had to be mean about it. After all, he was there doing Charlie a favor, so further aggravating the shopkeeper wasn't in the inn's best interests.

The man softened a bit from the question. "Cindy's fallback position is usually anger," he said with a grin, "and besides, she's not a big fan of Bear Creek at the moment. As for me, I just meant that we always load around back. I don't know about you, but I have no desire to carry the entire order from the back, through the store, and out into your truck. You are driving a pickup, aren't you?"

"We are," Alex admitted, still not sure that the man was being entirely honest with them.

"It's not one of those shortbeds with more seating space than cargo room, is it?" he asked Alex, clearly skeptical about the lighthouse innkeeper's ride.

"As a matter of fact, it's a beat-up old Ford longbed," Alex said with a grin. The bed itself was a full eight feet long, giving it its name, and Alex wouldn't have parted with it for three brand-new trucks side by side, though he never would have admitted it to anyone else, not even Elise. He'd spent a great deal of his life driving that pickup, and it meant nearly as much to him as the lighthouse itself. That was an exaggeration, and Alex knew it, but still, he was awfully fond of his truck, and woe to the person who mocked it.

"You're clearly my kind of guy," the mercantile owner said with a grin of his own. "I love old trucks, and longbeds are the best. So what if she has a few dents, a little rust, and a handful of scratches on her? That just gives her character, if you ask me. It sounds like we're in business," the man said. "Drive around back and we'll get you taken care of pronto."

Alex and Elise did as they were told, and after they moved their truck around to the loading dock, the man was already there waiting for them. After they got out of the truck and walked up the steps, the man stuck out his hand. "Sorry if we didn't welcome you properly before. It's just a little dicey around here since Clint died. My name's Sandy Hearns, by the way."

"It's nice to meet you, Sandy. I'm Alex, and this is my wife, Elise." He hadn't had that many opportunities to introduce Elise by her new title, and he never failed to grin when he said it.

"You're newlyweds, aren't you?" Sandy asked with the hint of a smile.

"How did you know?" Elise asked him.

"It wasn't that tough to tell. Your hubby couldn't keep from grinning when he introduced you. I remember feeling that way myself once upon a time."

"Is Sandy your real name, or is it a nickname?" Elise asked him.

He shrugged as he ran a hand through his remaining hair. "When I was a baby, my hair was the color of sand, and as thick as anyone could ever hope for. It didn't stay that way forever, and it's thinned out quite a bit over the years, but the nickname stuck. I don't mind a bit, given the fact that my given name is Beauregard Gale Hearns. I didn't pick them, and neither did my grandfathers, but there you go. One went by Bo, and the other answered to GT. Why my parents chose to saddle me with two names my own grandfathers didn't even like is beyond me, but what are you going to do?"

Sandy had become extremely talkative as opposed to how things had started out, and Alex had to wonder if it was because of Elise or his pickup. A great many men in the South judged others by what they drove. It might not have been fair, but at least this time it was working in Alex's favor.

As they started loading the order by hand, Alex asked him, "Did you know Clint Kidde well?"

"He was best friends with my son when they were growing up. In fact, he ate as many meals at my table as he did at his own," Sandy said. "That's why I think everybody around here is crazy."

"Why is that?" Elise asked him.

"There's no way Clint would ever kill himself. If you ask me, it had to be murder, plain and simple."

Chapter 8

"Murder? How could it have been murder?" Alex asked the storeowner as he stopped loading boxes and stared openly at the man. "He swallowed a lethal dose of poison."

"Maybe so, but it either wasn't done willingly, or he didn't know what he was drinking. Clint Kidde was a great many things, but a coward he was not, and if you ask me, suicide is nearly always a coward's path. Besides, Clint thought too much of himself to ever check out on his own. I can't imagine the scrap he could have gotten himself into that would make him do something like that."

Alex and Elise started loading boxes again, and as they worked, Elise asked him, "Does anyone else share that belief around here?"

"Just about everybody that counts, except for Chief Laughlin. The fact of the matter is that it's a lot easier to write it off as a suicide than it is to investigate what happened as a murder, and Willie Laughlin is three weeks from retirement. He wasn't all that great a police chief when he was worried about keeping his job, but now, he's barely showing up at all. He was only too happy to jump on the suicide theory, no matter how much Carver Ford and I argued with him about it."

"Who's Carver Ford?" Alex asked.

"He's a regular cop on the force, so there's only so much he can do, but if you ask me, he's a better lawman than Willie Laughlin ever dreamed of being."

"Do you all think Charlie Granger had anything to do with Clint's death?" Alex asked. He couldn't bring himself to call it murder, at least not until he had more information than he did so far, but Sandy seemed convinced that was what had happened to the painter.

"I don't know about that, but he was working for him, and you know how bosses and their employees can clash sometimes. Still, I'd have a hard time believing that Charlie did it," Sandy said.

"Then why refuse to make the delivery to Bear Creek?" Elise asked.

"That wasn't my fault. Barry Kidde is my driver, and he also happened to be Clint's cousin. It's a small town, you know. Most folks are family, if you go back far enough. Anyway, until Barry is satisfied that he knows the truth about what happened, he flat refuses to go out there. I can't leave the store, not with just Cindy and me working. It may be our off season for tourists, but that doesn't mean that it still doesn't take two people to run the place. How do you know Charlie?"

"We run an inn in the North Carolina Mountains," Elise said.

"That explains you pitching in on your honeymoon then. You guys stick together, don't you? Tell you what. I feel kind of responsible for you having to work, even if it was Barry's fault we didn't make the delivery. Come back after you drop off this order, and I'll take you both out to lunch, my treat."

"That's nice of you…" Elise started to say before Alex interrupted her.

"And we'd love to," he managed to get in before she could decline the invitation.

"Good enough. I'll see you in an hour, then," Sandy said after they moved the last box into the truck bed.

The mercantile owner started to go back in when Alex called him back out. "Hang on one second. I just need to check what we've got with the invoice, and then we'll be good to go."

Did Sandy frown for a second when he heard the news? Alex couldn't be sure, but suddenly, the storekeeper slapped his forehead with the palm of his hand. "I must be getting senile in my old age. I'm glad you spoke up. There were a few other things we forgot to load in back."

"It's easy to do," Alex said, happy that Charlie had warned

him to be vigilant. Alex didn't care for the storekeeper's principles, but that wouldn't keep him from taking him up on his offer to treat them to lunch.

"We'll see you soon," Alex said once he and Elise were satisfied that the order was correct.

"What was that all about?" Elise asked him as they headed back to the lodge.

"You were standing right there when Charlie told me to check the order before we left, and he was right," Alex explained.

"That's not what I'm talking about, and you know it. Why did you accept Sandy's lunch invitation?"

"How else are we going to hear more about why the entire town thinks that Clint was murdered?" Alex asked her.

"Are we investigating suicides now?" Elise asked him softly.

"I don't see that we have much choice if we're serious about helping Charlie. If we dig around a little and find out that it was a suicide after all, then maybe the town will stop freezing Charlie out."

"And if we discover that it was in fact murder?" Elise asked.

"Then we do our best to unmask the killer," he said.

"Even though the police chief is convinced that it was suicide."

"That may be true, but at least there's one cop on our side," Alex said. "If we can get Sandy to introduce us to Officer Ford, it might help him trust us enough to talk to us about his theories."

"I can't believe that we're investigating this on our honeymoon," Elise said as they neared the turnoff to the lodge.

"We don't have to if you don't want to," Alex said as he negotiated the poor excuse for a road they had to take back. "Tell me to drop it right now, and I won't say another thing about it the entire time we're here."

Elise seemed to think about his offer for a full minute

before she finally spoke. "No, we both know that we can't do that. If someone was murdered, the killer needs to be brought to justice, and if that means it's going to be a part of our honeymoon, then so be it."

Alex reached over and patted her leg. "That's how I feel, too."

"The question is, do we tell Charlie what we're up to, or do we do it covertly?"

"For the moment, I say we don't tell anybody," Alex said. "After all, we don't know who the real killer is, or even if it was murder at all."

"Do you think Charlie himself might have done it?" Elise asked him, clearly troubled by the idea.

"I have no idea," Alex answered, "but if he's involved in any way, I don't want him to know what we're up to."

"Agreed. Things are getting complicated, aren't they? I hope we have time to check out the gazebo before we have to head back into town for lunch."

"I've been curious about that, too," Alex admitted.

Elise nodded. "If the painter was spending most of his time there before he died, there might be a clue that everyone else missed."

"Did you have any trouble in town?" Charlie asked as soon as they returned.

As the newlyweds began to unload the order, Alex said, "It's all there, but it's a good thing I reminded Sandy about everything you asked for. The second I pulled out the invoice, he suddenly 'remembered' the rest of it, so we're good."

"Good old Sandy. I would have been shocked if you'd told me otherwise. Did he happen to say why Barry wouldn't make the delivery?" Charlie asked as they moved things into the lobby.

"It's understandable, given the fact that his cousin died out here," Alex said.

"He doesn't blame me for Clint killing himself, does he?"

Charlie asked as he put down another box.

"We didn't meet him, so you'd have to ask him that yourself," Alex replied, and he saw Elise nod in approval. It wasn't a lie by any definition, but it certainly wasn't anywhere close to the truth, either.

"I can't tell you how much I appreciate this," Charlie said as the last box was unloaded and the pickup was empty again. "Tell you what. I'll have Carrie whip us up something special for lunch, just the three of us."

"It's kind of you to offer," Elise said, "but Alex and I would love to head back into town and have a look around for ourselves. It is still our honeymoon, after all."

"Enough said," Charlie replied with a knowing smile. "Another time, then." Alex was unsurprised to see the innkeeper double-check the items after they had unloaded them. Given Sandy's propensity to "forget" parts of he order, he would have done the same thing himself. Once Charlie was satisfied, he nodded in approval. "You two are awesome. You know that, don't you?" the innkeeper asked with a grin.

"We try our best, and it wasn't that big a deal," Alex said. "Now, if you don't mind, we thought we'd take a quick stroll down to the gazebo before we head back into town to look around."

"Be my guest. I have to warn you, though. Clint only painted some of it. I'll have to do the rest myself when I get the chance. Now, before you get any ideas, I don't want you two offering to finish painting it for me, do you understand?"

"Trust me, that's not going to come up," Alex said. "Our lighthouse needs to be repainted, but you won't see either one of us lifting a brush to do it." He'd been teasing, not about Hatteras West's need of a fresh coat of paint but about the very idea that he and Elise could tackle such an enormous project on their own.

"I get it. Believe me," Charlie said. "I'll catch up with you two later, then. I need to get some of these supplies to Carrie pronto so she can get started on tonight's feast."

"We could hang around and help you move them," Elise volunteered.

"Thanks, but I have a luggage cart that works perfectly. Go on, you two. Have a little fun while you're here."

As Alex and Elise took the path to the gazebo, Elise asked her husband, "That discussion about painting made me wonder about something. Do you think we'll ever be able to afford to paint the lighthouse?"

"I don't see how," Alex admitted. He'd gotten a price quote once when the lighthouse on the coast had received a fresh coat of paint, but unless they won the lottery, it would be beyond their reach. Then again, maybe Emma would find a new vein of precious stones somewhere on Winston land and they could make it happen. It had occurred before, so it was within the realm of possibility, but Alex wasn't going to hold his breath.

"Wow, it's really pretty, isn't it?" Elise asked as they came out of the woods and into a clearing. The mountain lake came almost as a surprise, since it was so unexpected given the otherwise wooded surroundings. There was a small lake on Winston land near the inn, but it was nothing compared to this majestic body. The water looked green to Alex, and he wondered if it was because of the actual property of the liquid or the surrounding trees that lined the banks. Whatever the reason, it was lovelier to Alex than any ocean ever could be. As promised, there was indeed a small peninsula where the gazebo had been placed perfectly, allowing eight to ten people to sit under its copper-paneled roof and enjoy the view. Three-quarters of the wooden structure had been painted bright white, and the rest of the exposed wood had been sanded carefully and was ready to take on fresh paint itself.

Alex ran a hand along the sanded wood. "Clint did good work," he said. "Dad always said that the true test of a good paint job was the quality of the prep work."

"Alex, seeing this makes me think that it was murder after

all, just like Sandy said," Elise said as she slumped down onto one of the bench seats.

"Why do you say that?"

"Look around. It's clear by the amount of pride Clint took in his work that he wouldn't leave something partially finished, no matter what the circumstances might be. If you were doing this job, would you leave it unfinished for any reason?"

"I'm not the right person to ask, since I'm about as far from being suicidal as you can be," Alex admitted, but after a moment's thought, he added, "but you make a good point. Look at the way he cut in the corners, being sure to get paint even in the smallest spaces." Alex looked around. "Added to that, there's not a bit of splatter anywhere, either on the floorboards or the grass around it. He even stacked up his used drink bottles over there nice and neat. I see what you're saying."

Elise looked around. "Do you think there's anything here that might tell us what really happened to him?"

Alex glanced at his watch. "I don't know, but we don't really have much time to search right now. We need to get back into town. If Sandy is right—and it's beginning to look that way to both of us, regardless of what the police chief might think—we're going to need his connections with the locals if we're going to get anyone to speak with us."

"I agree, but we really do need to come back here after we're finished in town. Agreed?"

"Agreed," Alex said, and the two of them headed back down the path to the parking lot so they could go into town and see what they might be able to uncover there. They had a date with the storeowner, and Alex hoped that it might lead to more information than what they already had, which wasn't all that much anyway. That was the way it was with their investigations. Facts and theories seemed to come in piecemeal until at last, everything fell into place.

Chapter 9

"I know Joe's place doesn't look like much, but they have the best burgers in five counties right here," Sandy said proudly as he looked around the place. He clearly couldn't have been any prouder of it if his name had been on the deed.

Alex looked around the diner, and he had to smile. It reminded him a little of Buck's Grill, the diner in Elkton Falls where he and Elise loved to eat, not necessarily by its décor but by its atmosphere. He doubted a tourist would be impressed with the faded linoleum floors or the cracked vinyl booths, but to Alex, it felt like a little piece of heaven. The sweet tea they'd ordered had given credence to Sandy's claim that the place had good food. Alex had rarely found a diner or grill that didn't serve food on par with its tea, and if what he was currently drinking was any indication, this meal was going to be a home run.

"How are the fries?" Elise asked as she studied the menu.

"Home cut in back, and if it's possible, they're even better than the burgers are," Sandy said.

An older woman wearing galoshes and a plastic rain hat came up to their table looking agitated about something. "Have you heard the news, Sandy?"

"What's that, Evvie?" he asked her.

"There's going to be a flood," she said, looking frightened by the prospect.

"I heard that announcement, too," Sandy said, clearly trying to ease the older woman's fears. "It's just a flash flood warning. That doesn't necessarily mean that we're going to have one."

"You mark my words," she said as she pointed a bony finger in his direction. "When my rheumatism starts acting up, it's about to rain, and I mean by the bucketload."

"Then you'd better get home where you're safe and sound. You don't have anything to worry about once you're there, not sitting on top of the hill like you are," Sandy told her. "Believe you me, that's exactly where I'm going, and if you had any sense, you'd do the same yourself."

"Hey, Evvie. Looks like you're getting ready for some rain," a waitress in her mid-thirties said with a smile as she looked the older woman over.

"It's coming. You mark my words," Evvie said as she stormed off, no doubt heading for home and high ground.

"Are you all ready to order?" the waitress asked them after the woman was gone. She had on a nametag that said, "Call me Colleen," so Alex was determined to do just that.

"I don't know. Are we ready, folks?" Sandy asked Alex and Elise. Once they both nodded in the affirmative, the shopkeeper said, "Colleen, I'll have a double cheeseburger and a side of fries. Don't forget to make it all the way, darlin'," he added.

"As if you'd eat a burger any other way," Colleen said with a practiced grin. "How about you folks? I haven't seen you around town before."

Sandy explained, "Colleen here is the town welcome wagon. If you haven't been welcomed by her, then you haven't been properly welcomed at all."

"Sandy, don't you ever get tired of hearing yourself talk?" she asked with a grin before turning back to Alex and Elise. "Never mind him. He's mostly harmless."

"It's the 'mostly' part that gets me in trouble every time, though," the storeowner said.

"I'll have the same thing he's having," Elise said.

Alex handed her the menu back and smiled. "Make it three. It's nice to meet you, Colleen."

"Right back at you. You folks are making my life easy. I appreciate that."

"Glad we could help," Sandy said. "They're staying at the Bear Creek Lodge."

Colleen tensed up for just a moment before the artificial smile jerked back into place. "How nice for them," she said curtly.

"They were asking about Clint," Sandy pushed her. Alex thought the man had lost his mind. It was clear that Colleen didn't like the fact that they were guests of Charlie's, and now he was fanning the flames by mentioning the dead townie. "I told them both that there was no way on earth Clint drank that poison on purpose."

"And it's not likely he did it by accident, either," Colleen said. "You folks watch your step out there. There's just something's not right about that place."

"Are you having one of your premonitions, Colleen?" Sandy asked her. Alex thought he might be joking, but the waitress returned the question with a deadly serious expression.

"No, I haven't had a sight about it. It's just a feeling."

"Those count, too," Sandy said, and Colleen left them to fill their order.

"Does she really believe that she's psychic?" Alex asked Sandy softly once the waitress was gone.

"She doesn't just think it, Alex. She truly is." Sandy made the statement as though he were talking about the price of a dozen eggs instead of something so outlandish as clairvoyance.

"I'm curious about something. You seem convinced, so I'm wondering what premonitions has she had before?" Elise asked the question without a hint of mocking in her voice.

Sandy accepted the inquiry at face value. "When little Jason Masterson got lost in the woods, Colleen led a team straight to him after no one else could find the tyke. He was a good three miles from where he should have been, but Colleen didn't even hesitate. When Amanda Lancing lost her engagement ring, it was Colleen who found it buried in the onions where Amanda had been digging two days before, and when a big storm came through eight months ago, Colleen made everyone leave the post office, where they'd ducked into to get away from the rain. They all thought she was crazy, but it was easier retreating next door to town hall than it was to stand there and argue with her, she was so adamant.

Five minutes later, a tree came down from the storm and smashed that post office flatter than a pancake. Folks around here take her opinions pretty seriously, and you'd be wise to, as well."

Alex wasn't sure where he came down on the notion of clairvoyance. While it was true that some of those events could have merely been common sense, or Colleen might have been better at observing things that others missed, he wasn't ready to completely rule out that the woman actually had a gift that others lacked. The world was too big and a little too odd for Alex to completely discount anything.

"Did Colleen have any ties with Clint?" Alex asked after a few moments.

"They played coed softball together, and Clint dated her cousin, Maureen, for a few months five years ago. You know how it is. Shake a stick in a small town, and you're bound to find all kinds of connections."

"We're from a small place, too," Alex said. Though Elise hadn't been a local in Elkton Falls very long, she'd fit right into the community, and Alex had lived there all his life. He knew what Sandy was saying was true. There were often links, both exposed and hidden below the surface, between just about everyone in a tight-knit community.

"So then you get it," Sandy said, and then his face brightened. "Here we go. Prepare to be dazzled, folks."

Colleen brought them their food, and then she refilled their glasses with fresh tea before she left to take care of another table full of diners. Alex took his first bite and felt an explosion of flavors in his mouth.

Sandy had been watching him closely, and when Alex looked up at him, the storekeeper smiled. "I told you so, didn't I? What you're eating is grass-fed beef raised not ten miles from here, and Colleen's brother bakes the buns fresh every day in back. The veggies come from around here, too. No flash-frozen or preprocessed stuff for us around here."

"My question is why would anyone eat anywhere else?" Elise asked as she took another bite herself. "These fries are absolutely amazing."

"You bet they are. I know little Carrie Dale can cook, but can she do that?"

"That's right," Alex said between bites. "Carrie grew up around here, didn't she?"

"She moved away, but then she came back to town when her mama got older."

"That must mean that she knew Clint," Alex said. At that point, he was looking for any connection he could find between the folks at the inn and the dead man.

"Of course they knew each other," Sandy said. He left that hanging as he took another bite of his lunch, but Alex had a hunch that there was more there than Sandy was telling them.

"It was a little more than that, wasn't it?" he asked.

Sandy looked at Alex closely. "Why? What have you heard?"

"Nothing," Alex insisted.

"You don't have the sight yourself, do you?" Sandy asked him intently.

"No, sir, though I could see where it would come in handy. For example, I'm constantly misplacing the keys to my truck. It would be nice to know where they were at all times," Alex had said it to defuse the tension, but it backfired on him.

"It's not a laughing matter around here," Sandy said stonily. "We take gifts like that seriously."

Alex realized that he'd chosen the wrong time to use humor. "I'm sorry. I didn't mean anything by it."

The storekeeper accepted the apology, and then he started eating again.

"You didn't answer Alex's question," Elise said a few seconds later, apparently forgetting about her meal for the moment.

Had Sandy used Alex's joke as an excuse to change the subject? If so, he'd failed miserably. Once Elise got onto the trail of something, she was every bit as bad as Alex was about not letting it go until she found out the truth. It was one of the things he admired most about her, though the list was a long one, and it seemed to grow even longer every day.

"They went to prom together," Sandy mumbled, "but that was a long, long time ago. He dumped her right before they graduated, and it nearly broke the poor girl's heart. Some folks believe that was why she left town in the first place and buried herself in culinary school."

"That was a long time ago though, wasn't it?" Elise asked him.

"I don't know. It's all relative, isn't it? Bobby James stole my dessert in kindergarten, and I'm still sore about it every time I see him," Sandy said with a shrug. "You tell me, how much time is enough to let something go?"

"Who else out at the lodge had a connection with Clint?" Alex asked. His food was nearly gone, and he suspected so was his access to the wealth of local information. It was time to press on while he still could.

Sandy shrugged. "You know, Colleen's right. I do appear to be in love with the sound of my own voice. I kind of feel like a traitor telling outsiders our secrets."

It was meant to shut them down, but Alex and Elise weren't about to let that happen. "The truth is, we want what you want," Alex said softly.

"What might that be?" the shopkeeper asked cagily.

"To find out if Clint was murdered, and if he was, to make things right," Elise added.

"Pardon me for saying so, but what makes you think the two of you are capable of doing anything like that?" Sandy asked them skeptically.

"We've had a little luck with a few investigations of our own before," Alex admitted.

"So, are you saying you have a gift for it, like having a true sight?" Sandy asked him.

"Call it what you will, but all you really need to know is that we're good at it, if you trust us," Alex replied.

"Let me think on that a bit, if you don't mind," Sandy said quickly as Colleen showed up with three slips of paper.

"Here are your bills. You can pay up front if you'd like, or

I can take it for you, but the tips stay here," she said with a smile as she tapped the table.

"It's all on one check, Colleen," Sandy said.

"How did you connive your way into a free meal, Sandy Hearns?" Colleen asked as her gaze narrowed.

"I'll have you know that I'm hurt by that. As a matter of fact, I'm treating them to lunch today."

That clearly surprised her. "Why would you do something like that?" she asked suspiciously. "Something's not adding up, if you ask me."

"Barry won't make any deliveries to Bear Creek anymore, so these two had to do it for Charlie instead."

"That's nice of them, but it still doesn't explain why you're paying."

"They're on their honeymoon, Colleen," Sandy explained.

The waitress's smile lit up, this time clearly coming from the heart. As she looked at Alex and Elise, she asked, "Is that true?"

Alex held up his wedding band and grinned. "Yes, ma'am. It's brand new."

"Then you're all having dessert on me. We have the best apple pie you're ever going to eat."

"As much as we appreciate the offer, I'm not sure I could eat another bite," Elise explained.

"Deary, pie doesn't count. Ice cream on top, too, I think." She frowned for a moment, and then the waitress added, "You can have one too, Sandy. I want to do all I can to encourage this selfless behavior in you."

Colleen was gone before they could stop her, and Elise turned to Alex. "I'm not sure where I'm going to put it. It seems as though all we do on this trip is eat."

"I know what you mean, but I wouldn't feel right about turning down such a gracious offer," Alex said with a smile.

"That's you, Mr. Sensitive," she answered with a grin of her own.

"What can I say but it's true," Alex replied.

The three of them were waiting on their desserts when

Sandy pointed discreetly to a man eating alone. He wore a three-piece suit, had thinning brown hair, and looked as though he didn't have a friend in the world. "If Charlie had been murdered, my money would have been on Dexter Young over there," Sandy said softly.

"Why is that?" Alex asked as he studied the man.

"Dexter wanted the property, and he was about to get it when Charlie swooped in and stole it right from under him. Dexter's been keen on slamming Bear Creek Lodge ever since."

"Surely he wouldn't murder someone working there, would he?" Elise asked, clearly appalled by the idea.

Sandy just shrugged. "He never got along with Clint, so I wouldn't put it past him. No guests means no money, and unless I'm wrong, Charlie can't hold off too much longer running the place with so many vacancies."

"How do you know about that?" Elise asked him.

"Word gets around," Sandy said with a shrug.

"Not that specifically though, I'll wager," she pushed. "Has Carrie been talking about the situation out at the lodge?"

"I don't know where I heard it first, but you should know yourself that rumors are easy enough to get started. Besides, I deliver his food orders, remember? Don't you think I know when he's got a full house and when he's barely limping along?"

It was a valid point, and one that Alex hadn't considered. The storekeeper was in the perfect position to know just how much food was being consumed at the lodge, and from that, it was simple enough to figure out what the diminishing orders meant.

The pie and ice cream came, and Colleen made a big fuss over delivering it. "I wish nothing but the best for you both," she said. "A wedding means hope, at least as far as I'm concerned, and promise." She mumbled something under her breath, and then she smiled. "Be happy."

"What did she just say?" Alex asked Elise after the waitress was gone.

"I don't know. I didn't catch it," Elise said.

"It was a blessing from the old country," Sandy said. "She must like you. I've never seen her do that for outsiders before."

Alex knew how to respond to that. "You can get the check, but the tip is ours. I want to show Colleen our appreciation, for everything."

Sandy nodded, pleased with the request, and the three of them quickly consumed their treats, despite Elise's earlier protests of being too full to eat another bite.

After Alex left an extravagant tip, Sandy paid the bill, and they were soon out on the sidewalk together. Alex was about to thank the man for lunch again when someone approached them from behind.

When Alex turned to see who it was, he saw a man in a cop's uniform hurrying toward them, and he didn't look happy with any of them at the moment.

Chapter 10

"Hello, Chief," Sandy said, standing his ground as the older man nearly barreled into him. "It's a beautiful day, isn't it?" "Stuff it, Hearns," the police officer said, ignoring Alex and Elise completely. Alex was used to being ignored, but he'd never seen a man dismiss his bride so completely without even giving her a second look. "You've been shooting your mouth off all around town again, haven't you?"

"I won't deny it. Why, just this morning I discussed the price of beans with Benjamin Smith, and later, Sheila Montgomery and I had the most fascinating conversation about blue moons and why they weren't really blue at all." If the storekeeper was worried about the police chief's confrontational attitude, he didn't show it.

"You know what I'm talking about, so stop dancing around it. You're going around spreading rumors that Clint Kidde was murdered! You need to stop doing that before I lock you up!"

The man was so angry that spittle was flying from his lips, and Sandy made an exaggerated motion to wipe it from his face. "Say it, don't spray it, Willie."

"You are to address me as Chief Laughlin! Do you understand me?" he nearly screamed. The chief pulled a pristine white handkerchief from his pants pocket, dislodging two dimes, a penny, a black button, a few pieces of wrapped hard candy, and the brightest red paperclip Alex had ever seen in his life.

"I'll call you whatever you want me to, but why should I quit talking about what really happened?" Sandy asked, clearly getting a little angry now himself. "Everybody in town knows that Clint didn't kill himself."

"Not anybody who knows all of the facts," the police chief said. "I say it was intentional, and that's the way it's going to stand."

"You can wish that to be the case all you want to, but that still doesn't make it true," Sandy said angrily.

"What else could it be? Clint even mixed it in some fruity sports drink so he wouldn't taste the poison," the police chief insisted.

"What did he say in his note, Chief? Suicides generally leave those behind, don't they?" Sandy asked, the mocking tone in his voice obvious.

"You know as well as I do that there wasn't any note," the police chief said, "but that doesn't mean a thing. There aren't always notes."

"Then let me ask you this. Did Clint Kidde ever not want to get the last word in during his life? He did not," Sandy said, asking and answering his own question. "If anybody would have left a note, he'd have been the one to do it."

"Answer me this then, smart guy. If it was murder, how did the killer get him to drink the poison? And what was he doing in an empty guestroom in the first place? Oh, I have one more question for you. Why would anyone want to kill Clint? He might not have been a sterling citizen, but nobody hated him that much, did they? Well? Can you answer any of those questions?"

"I don't have to," Sandy said triumphantly. "I'm not the chief of police. If you're too old and too tired to do the job, Willie, why don't you quit so Carver Ford can take over?"

"Over my dead body," Chief Laughlin said angrily.

"Careful what you wish for, Chief," Sandy said.

"Is that a threat?" Laughlin asked softly. It was clear that Sandy had pushed him beyond the point where he was going to take it anymore.

"No, sir," Sandy said, pulling back. Clearly even he knew that he'd gone too far in their argument.

The police chief looked satisfied with Sandy's retreat. "That's more like it. Now stop spreading lies and rumors, or I'll lock you up. Do you hear me?"

"Funny, now that sounded like a threat to me," Sandy said.

"No, sir, just consider it a promise. I may be stepping down soon, but for the moment, I'm still the police chief, and what I say goes."

Chief Laughlin didn't even glance in Alex or Elise's direction as he stormed off. In Alex's opinion, Sandy had more than held his own in the argument, but after it was over, the man was clearly shaken by the confrontation.

"Are you okay, Sandy?" Alex asked him.

"No, but those things needed to be said," the shopkeeper answered. "Sorry you had to witness that. It's ridiculous for two grown men to fight on the sidewalk like a couple of thugs, let alone the chief of police and a town councilman, but we've been butting heads for years. The fact is that Willie's a pretty decent cop, but he's got to get off his duff and investigate this before whoever did it gets away with murder."

"Come on. We'll walk you back to your store," Elise offered.

"Are you sure you should be seen with a rabble rouser like me?" Sandy asked, getting some of his starch back.

"We'll risk it," Elise said with a grin as she put her arm in his.

There was nothing Alex could do but follow them, not that he wanted to do anything else. He'd promised himself that once they were married, he'd back Elise on every play she ever made, and he certainly had no problem doing it now. He was sure the chief of police hadn't meant to, but he'd just given them both some valuable information about the specifics of Clint Kidde's demise. For one thing, they hadn't known that the poison had been concealed in a sports drink bottle. That meant that there was another theory that the police chief may have overlooked. Someone could have seen how hard Clint had been working, which was obvious from the state of the gazebo, and they'd taken the liberty of poisoning him without him even knowing it until it was too late. Alex had read about a case where certain rat poisons were nearly instantly fatal, and he had to wonder if that was what had happened to the painter. After all, there had been those empty bottles neatly stacked near the gazebo, so the killer would have been able to grab one easily enough, fill it with poison, and then give it to Clint, all the while looking innocent in the process.

That still didn't explain what he'd been doing in that guestroom by himself, though. If he'd been alone at all, that was.

He'd asked Charlie about it, but the innkeeper hadn't seemed all that interested in answering Alex's questions at the time.

The last question Sandy had brought up had been valid as well. Who had hated the man enough to kill him? Or was the crime even motivated by hate? What if Clint knew something damaging to someone else? Some folks had been known to murder to protect their secrets, and the deeper they dug into this death, the more secrets seemed to be coming to light.

The three of them got to the front of the store and found obviously waiting for them a young man in uniform, lean and sharp, in direct contrast to the police chief they'd just seen.

"Carver, what are you doing here?" Sandy asked lightly. "Were you looking for me? If you're going to arrest me for something, can I go inside and tell Cindy first? She'll wonder where I went if I don't show up."

"No, you're safe, at least from me. The chief is on a tear though, and he's looking everywhere for you. I thought I'd stop by and give you a head start if you wanted to make a run for it," the man said with a grin. He noticed Alex and Elise and nodded to them. "Hey, folks."

"Carver, I'd like you to meet Alex and Elise Winston. They're staying at Bear Creek, and what's more, they agree with us. They think Clint was murdered, too."

It was more than either Alex or Elise had admitted to anyone else just yet, though it was true they were both beginning to believe it.

"Take it easy on that talk, would you?" Carver asked softly. "As it is, I've got hall monitor duty at the school for all of this week, and as an added insult, the chief has me working with the crossing guard, too. If he hears I'm going against him openly, it's hard to imagine what he'll do to me."

"We know what we know, though. The truth won't be buried," Sandy said.

Cindy must have seen them all talking out front, and she joined them. "Hey, Carver," she said, ignoring the outsiders. "Sandy, there's a supplier on the line that claims you shorted him on your last payment."

"It's Terry Jenkins, isn't it?" he asked.

"How did you know?" Cindy replied.

"It wasn't all that hard to figure out. He shorted me on my last order, so I shorted him right back when it came time to pay the bill," Sandy said firmly.

"Well, you'd better talk to him right now, or I'm afraid there's going to be trouble," Cindy said as she went back into the store.

"Sorry, folks, but duty calls," Sandy said as he started to head back inside himself. Before he went through the door though, he paused and added, "You three should really talk."

"I'd be happy to, but I've got to run myself," Officer Ford said. "Oh, by the way, there's a storm coming, and we've had a lot of rain as it is, so there could be flash flooding on the low-lying areas. I'd be careful if I were you."

Before Alex could even offer another time for them to get together, he and Elise were standing there on the sidewalk, alone.

"That was interesting," Alex said.

"To say the least. It's looking more and more like murder, isn't it, Alex?" Elise asked him.

"I'm afraid so. That poison being in the same kind of sports drink bottle sealed it for me. It would have been too easy to dose the drink, and if it was as sweet as the last one I tried, Clint might not even have realized that he was being poisoned at all until it was too late to do anything about it."

"So, what do we do? Should we head back to the lodge? Carrie has a connection to Clint that I suspect goes beyond him dumping her in high school, and I'd like to ask her about it."

"Me, too, but what about Zinnia? She's local too, isn't she? And we don't even know about the guests staying there."

"Do you think one of them might have had something to do with it?" Elise asked him intently.

"I'm not sure, but I'd like a whole lot more information before we approach any of them with our suspicions."

"Agreed," Elise said. "So, who's on our list here in town?"

"I'd like to speak with Clint's cousin, Barry, first," Alex said. "He might have more reason not to go back to the lodge than just being spooked about what happened to Clint."

"Could he be involved?"

"There's only one way to find out," Alex said. "Let's go track him down and ask."

It didn't take nearly as long to find Barry Kidde as either one of them thought it might. In fact, they'd only gone a few steps from the front door when Alex pointed to a delivery van sitting in the parking lot. It had the store's name and logo on it, and from where they stood, Alex could see that someone was in the front seat. It appeared that the driver was taking a nap, a baseball cap pulled down over his eyes, shielding them from the sunlight.

At least that was all Alex hoped he was doing.

"Hey. Wake up!" Alex said loudly as he knocked on the glass. "Are you okay in there?"

"I'd be fine if you'd keep your voice down," the man said grumpily as he sat up in his seat and rubbed his eyes, knocking the cap off for a second before he readjusted it. "I haven't been getting much sleep lately, so I thought I'd catch a few Zs on my lunch hour." He didn't get out of the cab, but he did open the door to make having a conversation with him easier.

"It probably frees up your day when you don't have to make all of your deliveries," Alex said with a wry smile.

"Why would you say something like that?" Barry asked him with a frown.

"We took the supplies out to the Bear Creek today," Alex admitted.

"Good for you. I hope you're available tomorrow, and the next day too, because I'm never going back to that place," the man said as he stretched a little.

"We're sorry about your cousin," Elise said.

Barry seemed to sit up a little straighter the moment he noticed that she was there. It was a reaction Alex had grown to expect since he'd first met Elise. "Thank you, ma'am. Clint wasn't the best guy around, and he had more than his own set of flaws, but he didn't deserve to die that way."

"We spoke with your boss," Alex said. "He told us he didn't think it was a suicide and that you agree with him."

"Of course I agree," Barry said indignantly. "Clint would no more kill himself than he would put on a dress and dance in the town square. The man had an ego as big as the moon. Besides, we made plans to go hunting together over Thanksgiving, and there's no way that Clint would miss that willingly. It was his favorite thing to do, and he looked forward to it all year long."

"If you're right and he didn't kill himself, who might have wanted to see him dead?" Elise asked him.

"Believe me, I've been thinking about that ever since they told me that lie about what happened to him. As far as I can figure it, there are a handful of folks who might want to see him out of the picture. You didn't know him, did you?"

"No, we never met," Alex replied.

"Well, let me tell you something about my cousin. He was always looking for an easy paycheck, and he wasn't above bullying someone to get it. My mama used to call him an opportunist. If he saw an opening, he never hesitated jumping on it with both feet. I figure he must have pushed someone a little too far, and they decided enough was enough."

"Do you have any particular candidates in mind?" Elise asked him.

"A few. Everybody in town knows that Carrie Dale was never a fan, but things got even worse between them after graduation."

"That was a long time ago though, wasn't it?" Elise asked him. "Surely she still wasn't upset about what happened so long ago."

"You'd think not, but a week before he died, they had a blow-out fight at the lodge, at least that's what Clint told me. It seems old Carrie wanted to pick back up where they left off, but Clint just laughed in her face. The man was a fan of eighteen-year-old girls all his life, no matter how old he was himself. Carrie was a little long in the tooth for him, and he told her that, in great detail."

Wow. Alex couldn't believe the nice woman he knew from Bear Creek might be a killer, but then again, he also knew that people weren't always exactly who they seemed to be. And didn't poison fit into her specialty as a chef in an odd way? She'd bear looking into; there was no doubt in his mind about that. "Is there anyone else in particular you have in mind? How about someone from town?"

"Well, the truth of the matter is that Chief Laughlin never cared for him," Barry said. "If you ask me, he was downright giddy when Clint turned up dead."

"What did the police chief dislike about him?"

"You probably don't know it, but he has an eighteen-year-old daughter named Chloe. She's as pretty as a picture, but not the brightest bulb in the lamp, if you know what I mean. For Clint, it was a combination he couldn't resist, even though the chief threatened to kill him if he went near his daughter again."

"He must have had her late in life," Elise said, commenting on the police chief's age.

"Yes, he had Chloe with his second wife," Barry said.

"Sadly, Eileen passed away three years ago, and since then, father and daughter have been as close as two people can be."

"Is that it?" Alex asked.

Barry shrugged. "The truth is, I can't help thinking that it might have had something to do with his work at the lodge. We were having a beer two nights before he died, and Clint told me that he had a fish on the line, but he had to be careful how he was going to reel it in. I got the impression he found something out about someone out there at Bear Creek, but when I pressed him on it, he told me that it was too soon to talk about."

That was interesting indeed. Had Clint found something out about one of the guests and then decided to try his hand at blackmail? If so, he'd evidently chosen the wrong victim.

"We heard that Clint had been depressed lately," Elise said softly.

Barry popped out of the van in disgust and stood much too close to Elise for Alex's taste. "That's a boldfaced lie. Who told you that?"

"Charlie Granger," she admitted, backing up a step. Alex got between them without even thinking about it.

"Well, he would say something like that, wouldn't he?" Barry asked in protest.

Alex noticed that something had fallen out of the truck when Barry had gotten out so abruptly. It was a photograph of a group of people surrounding a fire pit. Alex leaned over to pick it up, but he barely had time to glance at it before Barry snatched it out of his hands.

"That's a nice picture. What was it, a family reunion?" Alex asked him.

"It was Maw-Maw's eightieth birthday party," he grumbled as he stuffed the photo into his shirt pocket.

"Why would Charlie lie about Clint?" Elise asked him. Alex knew that his wife wasn't about to be intimidated into not following up with another question.

"They didn't get along much. Truth be told, Clint was just looking for a reason to quit. Don't get me wrong. My cousin did good—careful work—but he found something out about Charlie that he didn't like." The deliveryman paused before adding, "Don't ask me what it was though, because I asked, and Clint wouldn't tell me." Barry stared at them both for a few seconds before asking, "What makes you two interested in this, anyway?"

"We're staying in the room next to where Clint's body was found," Alex said. It wasn't a great excuse, but it was the best one he could come up with on such short notice.

"Well, I'll say this for you. You're going to more trouble finding out the truth than most folks around here are. Listen, Clint might have been a pain in the rear, but he was family, you know?"

"We get it," Alex said as Sandy came out and rejoined them.

"Are you two still here? I figured you'd be back at the lodge by now," he said as he studied the scene.

"We were starting a walk around town when we noticed Barry," Alex explained.

"Were you sleeping in the van again?" Sandy asked him not unkindly.

"Sorry, boss," the man replied sheepishly. "It won't happen again."

"No worries. I just need you to run some things out to Barlow's Hollow on the double."

"I'm on it," Barry said, and then he nodded to Alex, and then he tipped his baseball cap to Elise.

"I'm sure I'll see you both around," Sandy said as Barry got into the van and backed it up to the loading dock. "After all, it's a small town."

"There's no doubt about it," Alex said with a slight smile.

Once they were alone again, Elise asked, "What's going on, Alex? You're acting as though you know something I don't, or am I just missing something?"

"It's not your fault. You didn't get a good look at the photo that fell out of the van," Alex said, feeling his excitement begin to surface about what he'd seen.

"Well, don't keep me in suspense. What was it?"

"I happened to catch a familiar face in the crowd at Maw-Maw's birthday party. You'll never believe who was there."

"Don't make me guess," she said.

"Helen Brisbane. Unless I miss my guess, she's not only from around here too, but she's related to Clint Kidde somehow. Funny how she never mentioned that to anyone, isn't it?"

"It could just be a coincidence," Elise said, though she was clearly as troubled by the prospect as Alex was.

"I don't believe that for one second, and neither do you," Alex said flatly.

"No, I don't. We need to speak with her as soon as we get back, don't we?"

"I'm just trying to decide if we should corner her first or go after Carrie or Charlie," Alex admitted.

"Carrie I understand, particularly if she and Clint just had a public argument, but do you really think Charlie could have killed the painter?"

"At this point, it's too soon to say, but we can't rule him out, either. We need more information," Alex admitted.

"I don't disagree, but I'm not sure where we can get any more."

"Zinnia's from around here. Maybe we should see if we can uncover anything about her."

"Alex, surely you don't suspect her of killing Clint."

"I don't know, Elise. She's not much older than eighteen herself, and she's a cute girl with lots of personality. Doesn't that sound like it matches the profile of someone Clint might go after?"

"Perhaps, but Zinnia wouldn't stand for it, based on what we've seen of her so far."

"I agree. But what if she rejected him, he took offense, and she felt trapped?" Alex asked her, trying to come up with a possible motive for the waitress/maid.

"I suppose it's possible," Elise admitted.

"Well then, let's go see what we can find out about her."

Chapter 11

The pair soon found that it was harder to find someone who was willing to speak with them without having Sandy there to vouch for them. Alex wasn't really all that surprised by it, though. After all, he knew that if a pair of strangers came to Elkton Falls and started asking questions, they'd most likely get blank stares, just as the two of them were currently getting. In his paranoia, Alex could swear that someone was watching their every move, but he knew how jumpy he got whenever he and Elise were investigating a crime, particularly murder.

"This is pointless," Elise said with a sigh. They'd tried the grocery store, the beauty shop, and two clothing stores, but evidently Zinnia was a phantom in town, which they both knew was patently false.

"Should we give up and head back?" Alex asked as he looked at the troubling sky above. "It looks like rain really is heading our way."

"Do you believe we might get flooded out?" Elise asked him.

"No, the lodge is on high ground, but the road to it certainly isn't. Evidently they've had a great deal of rain lately, and the ground must be pretty saturated as it is. It wouldn't take much."

"How do you know that? From a flash flood warning?" Elise asked. "I've heard everything that you've heard since we've been here, and that doesn't necessarily mean that they've had a ton of rain."

"Think about it. What did I notice that you didn't?" Alex wasn't being arrogant or even mean to her. It was a game they sometimes played, challenging each other intellectually. Alex usually came out on the short end, and it felt good to have noticed something that Elise had missed for once.

It took her less time than he thought it would. Within ten

seconds, Elise said, "You're talking about the bridge, aren't you? The water was already really high under it when we crossed over it today, so if we get much more rain, it could wash out."

"That's what I was thinking," Alex admitted. "What should we do about it, though? Should we leave the lodge and head back home before it gets too bad? I'd hate to get stranded out there, especially if there was a killer on the loose."

"I don't know," Elise said doubtfully. "A part of me says that's the prudent thing to do, but another part is screaming that if we don't find out who killed Clint Kidde, nobody else is going to even bother trying."

"Tell you what. Let's go back to Bear Creek and pack, just in case. We can slip our bags into the truck, and if things start to look dicey, we can make a decision at that point."

Elise looked at him oddly. "Honestly, I wasn't expecting that reaction from you."

"What were you expecting?" he asked her.

"In the past, you've been the one leading the charge when it came to investigating murder. It just surprised me, that's all."

Alex took in a deep breath and then let it out slowly before he answered. "In the past, I wasn't a married man. I have more to think about than just myself these days."

Elise frowned for a moment before she spoke. "Alex, what did I say when we got married? Nothing needs to change. What's more, it shouldn't. As much as I appreciate you being worried about my safety, I'm not about to let you wrap me up in cotton and put me on a shelf somewhere just so I won't get hurt."

"Bubble wrap," Alex said after a moment's hesitation.

"Excuse me?"

"I'd put you in bubble wrap, not cotton," Alex said.

"I'm not joking," Elise said firmly.

Alex nodded. "I know. It's just my way of saying that you're right, and I'm wrong. I have a hunch I'm going to be saying that a lot in our married life. Should I have a card printed up or something so I can just hand it to you whenever I say or do something stupid?"

Elise laughed, hugged him, and then she kissed him soundly. "I'm glad we found each other."

"So am I," Alex said when he felt a tap on his shoulder.

"Hey, no canoodling on the street, even if you are on your honeymoon," Colleen said with a grin.

"Why aren't you at the diner?" Alex asked her, a little embarrassed about getting caught kissing Elise in public. Usually they were pretty private people, limiting their public displays of affection, but for goodness sake, if he couldn't express his love for his wife on their honeymoon, when could he?

"Contrary to popular belief and Joe's express and devout wishes, I have a life outside of that place," she said. "What have you two been up to since you left Joe's?"

"The truth is that we've been asking questions that no one seems to want to answer," Alex said.

Colleen frowned, and her voice softened for a moment. "You're digging into what happened to Clint, aren't you?"

"Guilty as charged," Alex said. "We can't just let it go. If he was murdered, he deserves justice."

She took that in for a moment before speaking. "Well, what have you got so far?" she asked them.

After giving the waitress a brief rundown on their progress to date, Alex asked, "Do you know anything about Zinnia Frost?"

"Just about everything, I'd say," Colleen answered with a smile. "She's a good girl, and someday she'll be a fine woman. What do you want to know?"

The situation was awkward, but Alex needed to ask his question anyway. "How was her relationship with Clint Kidde?"

"Relationship? You're kidding, right? Zinnia wouldn't give him the time of day. There's no doubt about that in my mind."

"What if he pursued her even after she rejected him? We understand Clint liked eighteen-year-old girls," Elise said.

"Maybe so, but he wasn't all that fond of the ones that were smart enough to know better, and I'd definitely put Zinnia Frost in that category. An older boy in middle school tried kissing her once when she wasn't interested, and she broke his nose! Trust me, the message got around loud and clear not to mess with her."

Alex frowned. "Okay then."

"What did I just say?" Colleen asked, looking troubled by his reaction. "What's wrong?"

"Colleen, you just admitted that Zinnia has a history of reacting to unwanted advances with violence," Elise said softly.

"That's not what I meant," the waitress said, clearly flustered. "All I was saying was that she didn't put up with nonsense, and Clint knew it. There's no way he'd go after her. She was just too smart for his taste."

Alex nodded. "You're probably right."

"But you're still not sure you believe it, isn't that the truth? Here I was trying to help the poor girl, and I just dug a deeper hole for her. I'm beginning to see why folks around town have been reluctant to talk to you."

With that, the waitress walked away without another word.

Alex looked at Elise as he said, "We seem to make new friends wherever we go, don't we?"

His bride hugged him, and then she took his hand. "We always knew that we had to ask hard questions, Alex. It's the nature of what we do."

"Do you mean innkeeping?" he asked her with a smile.

"No, and you know it. I don't know about you, but I'm ready to head back," Elise said as a few raindrops started to splatter down on them.

"Race you back to the truck," he said.

By the time they got there, which was not more than a hundred yards away, they were both soaking wet. Instead of driving off, they sat in the front seat of the truck watching the rain pummel the hood of the truck and the ground around them. At one point, the noise was so loud that they couldn't speak without shouting. Then, as abruptly as it had come, it stopped, leaving the world around them glistening with the fresh moisture.

"We'd better head back," Alex said.

"To interview our suspects?" Elise asked him.

"Sure, but I'm worried about that bridge. I know that it's probably withstood dozens of storms worse than that one, but I don't want to risk it if we don't have to."

"I couldn't agree with you more," Elise said.

Alex waited until they'd crossed the bridge before he spoke again. The rain hadn't raised the waterline much, at least not from what he could see, but he was well aware that it was the runoff after the storm that often caused flash floods. "I still want to pack our bags and be ready to leave at a moment's notice."

"I've been thinking about it, too," Elise admitted. "Was it my imagination, or was that water climbing even farther up the side of the bridge?"

"I thought it was about the same, but then again, maybe it was wishful thinking on my part. So, what do you say?"

"Let's pack, but we won't say anything to anyone. If we can find a way to slip our bags into the truck without anyone else noticing, so much the better." Elise leaned over and kissed his cheek.

"Not that I'm complaining, but what was that for?" he asked her.

"I kind of like the fact that you're looking out for me," she admitted. "Don't stop, okay?"

"I promise I won't, at least as long as there is a single breath left in my body," he said.

To Alex's surprise, the Eastons were getting out of their car as he and Elise pulled up. Where had they been? Had the pair been following them back in town? Alex had written off the strange feeling that they'd been watched to paranoia, but maybe there really had been someone there.

"Did you enjoy your trip to town?" Alex asked the couple as he and Elise approached them.

"What? No. We weren't in town," Carlton said swiftly. "We were nowhere near it."

"We were hiking," Val volunteered a little too loudly. Judging by the clothes they were wearing and the pristine condition of their shoes, Alex doubted it, especially since the area had been subjected to so much rain recently.

Carlton must have noticed Alex's attention to their feet. "What can I say? She thinks walking half a block on a city street is hiking. We weren't 'hiking' hiking like looking for bears in the woods or anything like that," he said. "We just went for a stroll. But not in town."

"Do people actually go out in search of bears?" Elise asked him.

"Why wouldn't they? After all, it's in the name of this place. We thought there might be some around, so we drove a while, got out and looked around, and then drove some more. How about you two?"

"No, we haven't been out looking for bears, or any wildlife at all, for that matter," Alex said.

"I didn't think you were. Did you two enjoy town? I assume that's where you went, since you both keep mentioning it. Did you?"

"We did," Elise said. "Thanks for asking. You two were here when the painter died. Did you have any contact with him?"

They both shook their heads instantly. "No, not to say hello to or anything. Why, did someone say that we did?" Val asked suspiciously.

"No, I was just curious," Elise replied.

"Well, we have to go get ready," Carlton said. "It will be time to eat soon enough."

The two of them retreated inside the lodge, but Alex held Elise back for a moment so they could have a private word. "Was it me, or were they just acting really weird?" he asked her.

"They're clearly up to something," Elise said. "I'm just not sure what it might be."

"You know, I wasn't going to mention it, but seeing them made me think of it again. I had the strangest feeling that someone was following us in town. Did you?"

"I thought I was just being jumpy, but I felt it, too," Elise agreed. "Did you get a good look at whoever it was?"

"No, it was more of a sensation than an actual sighting," Alex admitted.

"Well, I'm certainly not taking the Eastons off our list after that little show they put on."

"Neither am I," he agreed. "Who do we tackle first?"

"Unless I miss my guess, Charlie should be the easiest one to locate," Elise said. She must have noticed Alex's frown, because she added, "You hate thinking that a fellow innkeeper might have done it, don't you?"

"I know it's not rational, but we're cut from the same cloth, you know?"

"Alex, we can't judge him based on what he does for a living. He has two strikes against him, as far as I'm concerned."

"You're right. He's the only one who mentioned that Clint had been depressed lately. That would be a good smokescreen if he was trying to cover up a murder."

"And the two of them had a fight, at least according to Barry Kidde," Elise added.

"The question is, can we believe Barry?"

"I think so," Elise said after a moment of thought. "He didn't try to sugarcoat the kind of man his cousin was, but he clearly cared about the man despite how well he knew his flaws."

"Okay, you're right," Alex said. "Let's go talk to Charlie."

"About what?" a voice asked, coming from the direction Alex and Elise had just driven past. "I saw you drive in, but you must have missed me."

"Were you out near the road?" Alex asked him.

"I was checking out the bridge," he admitted. "These storm warnings have me a little jumpy, so I wanted to make sure it was still okay."

"And is it?" Elise asked.

"It's solid as ever. That bridge has withstood a lot worse. We're going to be fine unless the creek floods over the top of it, and I've never seen that happen since I've been here. What did you want to talk to me about?"

"We had several conversations while we were in town, and we discovered a few things that troubled us," Alex said.

"We were hoping you could clear things up," Elise added.

Charlie frowned. "Let me guess. You talked to some of the conspiracy theorists about Clint's death. They think it was murder, don't they?"

"As a matter of fact, they do," Alex admitted, though he didn't add the fact that he and Elise believed the same thing as well. "You seem to be the only one who noticed that Clint was depressed."

"So? I was also around him the most." Charlie looked hard at both of them before he added, "You believe me, don't you?"

"Why wouldn't we? There's no reason for you to lie about it, is there?" Alex asked. "How did you two get along, in general, I mean?"

Charlie shook his head in disgust. "That's why I hate going into town. They've already created a murder where there was none, and now they're hanging me without a trial. Why am I not surprised?"

"Is it true, though, at least the essence of it?" Elise asked him gently.

"Clint worked for me. We had a few disagreements, but is that really all that odd? I didn't kill him, and neither did anyone else. He took his own life."

"Why was he in number seven?" Elise asked him. "Didn't that strike you as odd? Alex asked you about it before, but you just brushed him off."

Clearly Charlie had hoped that the interrogation was over,

but when he realized that it wasn't, he decided to talk. "He'd been having trouble sleeping, so I gave him a key so he could grab a nap on his lunch break," the innkeeper said. "There was nothing mysterious about him being there."

"And what about the poison? We heard it was delivered in a sports drink bottle," Alex said. "It was the brand he liked to drink, wasn't it?" It was a hunch, but one based on firm ground.

"So what? I doubt he would have gulped the poison down straight from the container. Besides, if he tried to walk through the lodge with a can of rat poison, I believe someone might have stopped him, or at least commented on it."

Their questioning wasn't working, and Alex knew it. He had to get Charlie back on his side if they were going to be able to move freely around the resort questioning people. "I just have one more question. Say you're right, and Clint took his own life. What's your theory about what really happened?" he asked.

"If you ask me, Clint had probably been carrying that bottle around with him for days. It was his drink of choice, and when he emptied it, he loaded it up with poison, just in case. Who knows how long he toted it around? I think he went upstairs to take a nap, and when he couldn't get to sleep, his troubles overwhelmed him, and he finally decided to end his misery. Have you ever been sleep deprived? I went through a bout of it in college, and I was ready to jump into traffic after four days of being awake practically around the clock. It does things to your mind, and it makes you do things you wouldn't ordinarily do. Anyway, that's what I think."

"You could very well be right," Alex said, noticing Elise's eyebrows rise as he said it. He'd have to share his strategy with her later. For now, he believed that they'd found out all they could from the innkeeper.

"Listen, I need to check on some of the outbuildings, just in case we get another storm. I'll see you inside," Charlie said, and then he walked away.

Alex and Elise both nodded, and after the man was gone,

Elise asked, "What was that all about?"

"He wasn't going to tell us anything else," Alex said. "I decided that we needed him to at least think that we believed him."

"We don't though, do we?"

"The jury is still out, at least as far as I'm concerned. Elise, everything we discover makes me realize that either scenario could work. It might have happened exactly as Charlie just laid out."

"Then again," Elise said, breaking in, "whoever killed him could have known about his habit of drinking that particular brand and dosed it so he wouldn't be suspicious until it was too late."

"Wheels within wheels within wheels," Alex said. "Let's go have a chat with Carrie before she gets too busy with dinner."

"Lead the way," Elise said, and they reentered the lodge to grill another suspect in a murder no one there seemed to want to admit had even happened in the first place.

Chapter 12

"Carrie, do you have a second?" Elise asked the chef as they entered the kitchen. Alex and Elise had agreed that she'd take the lead in questioning the woman, since Elise could project a more sympathetic front than Alex could ever seem to manage. He looked around the facility and was surprised to see so much new equipment everywhere. It must have cost Charlie a fortune to outfit it.

"Sure. The chicken's marinating, so I have at least ten minutes until I have to move on to the next step. I missed you two at lunch."

The question wasn't accusatory, but it was definitely probing.

"We ate in town," Alex admitted.

"At Joe's, I hope?" she asked. "I just love their burgers. I've been after him ever since I got back for his secret seasoning mix, but so far, he won't tell me."

"The burgers were truly awesome," Alex said, and then Elise tilted her head as she looked at him. He knew that she needed to take over, but it was hard for him to sit back and watch someone else lead, even if it happened to be his own wife.

"They're so good, I eat there on my day off," Carrie said.

"How's your mother doing?" Elise asked, surprising Alex with the question. They hadn't discussed how she'd approach the chef, and it had caught him off guard.

"How do you know about that?" she asked the pair.

"We heard someone mention it in town," Elise replied, keeping it vague enough to be accepted.

"She has good days, and then there are bad ones, too," Carrie said.

"It was really special of you to come back here to take care of her," Elise said.

"Thanks, but she's the one who really deserves the credit.

My mother was wonderful when I was growing up. Coming back home to take care of her was the least I could do."

"Still, it must have been hard returning, what with all of the memories still around about why you left in the first place." The statement had been handled deftly, and Alex found himself admiring Elise's subtle approach.

"You two have been busy, haven't you? Let me guess. You talked to Colleen. No, she wouldn't share that. Sandy. Yes, it had to be him."

"There was talk," was all that Elise would admit. "I can't imagine how difficult it was having Clint around all of the time after what happened between you."

"It wasn't that big a deal. So he dumped me at graduation. People get rejected every day. It was so far in the past I can barely remember anything about it."

Even Alex, not normally that adept at reading women, knew that Carrie was lying. "So, you two didn't argue in public recently?" he asked, forgetting himself for a moment.

Carrie stared at him a moment before speaking, and when she did, tears started to creep down her cheeks. "Go ahead, mock me. I thought we might be able to go out and grab a bite to eat, nothing serious, you know? He just laughed in my face. He said I was old news and that he only went after fresher editions. I slapped him, he laughed about it, and then I avoided him until the day he died. Do I regret what happened? Of course I do! He wasn't a great guy, and he did me a favor by turning me down, but I should have been nicer to him when he was alive, and I'll probably take that to my grave."

Alex wasn't sure about Elise, but he certainly believed the chef. She was too convincing for him to think otherwise.

Clearly Elise wasn't quite so sure.

"When was the last time you saw him?" she asked.

"It was the day before he died, when I went home for the night. Clint was hanging around the lodge after he finished, but I knew it wasn't to see me. I'd been coming down with something all day, so I stayed home the next day, which was when he died. Thank goodness for that. I don't know how I would have reacted seeing them cart his body away."

"If you weren't here, then who cooked in your place?" Elise asked her.

"Maggie Gray came in to sub. She's serviceable, but she was in over her head. Charlie pled for me to come back, and I toughed it out and was back at my station two days later, though I didn't feel all that great for a while." A timer went off, and Carrie said, "Excuse me, but if we're going to eat on time, I have to get busy."

Alex thought they were leaving, but Elise lingered for a moment as she said, "I'm sorry if we dredged up old wounds. Your food really is spectacular."

"I never get tired of hearing that," she said, doing her best to smile.

"Are we good?" Elise asked.

"We're fine," Carrie said, and to Alex's surprise, the chef then hugged his wife. "I appreciate you coming back and talking to me. It gets lonely with just my mom and me, and when I'm at work in here, I'm usually by myself all of the time."

"Well, as long as I'm here, I'll be pestering you, and not just for recipes," Elise said.

"I'd like that."

Once they were out in the hallway, Alex said, "So, it appears that we can take Carrie off our list."

"Unless she tainted the drink the day before, and her sickness was just a convenient way to distance herself from the scene of the crime," Elise replied with a frown.

"Wow, I never even considered that as a possibility. You're pretty amazing."

"I manage, but you tend to ask better questions than I do."

"Don't sell yourself short," he said. "You were great, and not just with the way you spoke with her. You make a connection with everyone you meet, don't you?"

"I suppose so. It comes from growing up in an inn," she

said dismissively.

"We both know that's not true. Don't forget, I grew up in one, too."

She chuckled lightly. "Alex, you're good with people, too."

"I used to think so, until I met you. I'm just wondering if you give lessons, and where do I sign up for the course?"

That delighted her, for some reason. "Don't change too much. I love you just the way you are. Now, unless I miss my guess, that's Zinnia's maid cart I hear rolling around on the second floor. Let's go see if we can steal a moment of her time."

"Zinnia!" Elise said loudly for the third time, this time tapping the maid directly on the shoulder to get her attention. The young woman was sweeping the hallway, and she had buds in her ears, evidently listening to music as she worked.

"What's going on? Hey, Alex, Elise. You nearly scared me out of my skin," she said as she pulled both buds out so she could hear them.

"Do you have a second?" Elise asked.

"I've got so much work to do, I don't have time to change my mind. I'm trying to do three people's jobs, and it's killing me."

"How about if I sweep while you talk to Elise?" Alex volunteered. Even though he was on his honeymoon, he'd already proven that he wasn't above getting his hands dirty.

"You don't have to do that," Zinnia said, though clearly she could use the break.

"I insist," Alex said as he gently pried the broom out of her hands.

As he got to work, Zinnia grabbed a seat from the hall and sat down. "Thanks. I appreciate that. What do you want to know?"

"It's about Clint Kidde," Elise said.

Zinnia started to get up again. "Break's over. Sorry."
Elise stood close enough to the chair to make it awkward for

Zinnia to stand, and the maid abruptly sat back down again. "I don't have anything to say about him, now or ever," she insisted, "and you can hover over me until dinner for all I care."

"Did he make a pass at you before he died?" Elise asked her. "It's okay if he did. It wasn't your fault."

"Don't you think I know that? Sure, he tried to get me a few times, but I bit him, and hard, and after that, he started avoiding me."

"You actually bit him?" Alex asked, his broom hovering momentarily as he asked the question.

Zinnia grinned. "Not literally. I simply made a few observations, mostly about why a man his age would go after a girl mine. I asked if perhaps it was because he wasn't ready to take on a grown woman, so he tried to find ones he could impress, like Chloe or Cynthia, the poor dim dears. Needless to say, Clint didn't care for my comments, I can tell you that."

"Did he ever actually lay a hand on you?" Elise asked. Alex knew why she was asking, since they'd heard about Zinnia's past temperament.

They didn't have to bring it up, though. She did it for them. "Ever since I punched Tommy Harpold in the nose for grabbing me from behind, I haven't had many problems with unwelcome advances. It's amazing how folks can pick up on things like that."

Alex was finished with his sweeping, and what was more, he was satisfied with Zinnia's story. Maybe she had been involved in Clint's murder, but for the moment, he was going to give her the benefit of the doubt. He was about to fetch the dustbin from the cart to collect the debris he'd amassed when he spotted two master keys on top, both clearly marked with little paper tabs. One was partially obscured by a room-cleaning schedule, and without giving it another thought, Alex deftly picked it up and slid it into his pocket. He wasn't exactly sure how he was going to use it, but he knew that he'd rather have it than not.

Alex was surprised to discover that not only had the maid gotten up, but she was standing right behind him. Had she seen him take the key? If so, he wasn't sure how he could explain his actions.

Instead, she said, "You know, it's nice watching a man work around the inn."

"Doesn't Charlie help out?" Alex asked, trying not to give away what he'd just done.

"Oh, he tries, but clearly your hands are no strangers to domestic work. No offense intended," she added.

"None taken," Alex replied, smiling with relief that he'd made the snatch without being caught.

"I know what you mean," Elise said as she hugged her husband from the side. "Cleaning is more appealing than most men realize, isn't it?"

"I'll second that," Zinnia said, and then she glanced down at her watch. "Oh, no, I'm late. I've got to set up for dinner service tonight."

"We can finish up for you upstairs if you'd like," Alex volunteered. It would give them a chance to spy on their fellow guests, and besides, Alex and Elise often worked side by side cleaning whenever they had the chance.

"Charlie would fire me on the spot if I let you do that," she said. "Let me just push this cart into number two, and then I'll be on my way."

Alex was relieved that she hadn't chosen one of the other empty rooms on the floor like number seven, where Clint had been murdered.

Zinnia didn't even notice the missing key, at least not at the moment. Alex would do his best to return it without her knowing about his actions if he could manage it. After all, there was no reason to get her in trouble for something that he'd done.

After the maid was gone, Elise looked at him oddly. "There's that grin again. What have you done, Alex?"

"I thought we might have a look around number seven before anyone sees that I grabbed this off Zinnia's cart," he said as he dangled the stolen master key in the air.

"You actually stole that?" Elise asked, her voice elevating slightly as she asked him the question.

"I like to think of it more along the lines of borrowing it," Alex explained. "You don't have to go in with me, but I would appreciate it if you'd play lookout for me while I check the place out. I have a hunch that whatever the killer was looking for, he or she hasn't found it yet."

"Alex Winston, if you think you're going to search that room without me, you've clearly lost your mind," Elise said with a grin.

"Then let's do it, but we have to be quick. We can't afford to let anyone else know what we're up to."

"What are we waiting for, then? I'm ready if you are," Elise said, and a moment later, they were inside.

Chapter 13

"How should we tackle this?" Elise asked Alex, her voice in a near whisper.

"You're going to have to speak up if you want me to be able to hear you," he said with a smile. "If we use our normal indoor voices, we should be fine as long as we keep the door closed."

She laughed softly. "Okay, you're right. The question stands, though. Should we come up with a system or just start digging in?"

"At first I thought we'd just snoop around, but why don't you start in here and I'll take the bathroom? We have one advantage over whoever tossed the place yesterday," he said.

"What's that?"

"We work in guestrooms all day, every day," he replied. "Think about all of the hiding places we have at Hatteras West."

"Don't get me started," Elise said with a slight frown. "I'm already homesick for our place. Am I being ridiculous?"

"No, ma'am, at least not as far as I'm concerned. I miss it, too. Come on, I'm not sure how much time we have."

"Then let's get to it."

Alex headed for the bathroom while Elise tackled the main space. He doubted he'd have to spend much time in the small area, and as he'd just told his bride, knowing his way around couldn't hurt.

After five minutes, he drew a complete blank. If there were any clues hiding there, he hadn't been able to find them.

"Any luck?" he asked Elise as he rejoined her.

"Not yet."

"Okay. I'll start on the closet, and then I'll help you."

"Alex, I don't have much more to search," she admitted. "What if there's nothing here for us to find?"

"Then we cross the room off our list and move on," Alex

said as he tackled the small closet. There was a luggage holder inside, something he and Elise had been talking about adding to the rooms at Hatteras West. It was light, easily collapsible, and it offered the perfect space to hold a suitcase. Lifting it up to see what the brand name was, Alex was surprised to see something stuck under one of the legs.

"Elise, I may have found something," he called out as he stepped back out of the closet.

"Me, too. Zinnia might be a wonderful young lady, but she lacks something in the cleaning department. Has she even run a vacuum in here?" Elise asked as she held her hand out. In it were torn pieces of a receipt from the lodge, a handful of sunflower seed shells, three pieces of plastic wrapping the size of a sugar packet, and a quarter that had been coated in something sticky. It was covered in lint, and Elise started to throw everything away when Alex said, "Let's keep it."

"It's probably just flotsam and jetsam from a dozen different stays, Alex," she said.

Alex pulled out his bandana, and she deposited her finds anyway. "You're probably right, but you never know," he said with a shrug as he put it away. "I hit the jackpot in the closet."

"What did you find?" she asked him eagerly. They were both into the spirit of the hunt. Even though it had been motivated by a tragic act, that didn't mean that they couldn't get fully involved in their quest for the truth.

"It's a note of some kind. Can you read what it says?"

"'eet me at the Gaz,'" she read aloud. "And then below it, it says, ':30.'"

"I know. It's not much of a clue, is it?"

"Are you kidding? I think you've got something here. Someone, maybe the killer, wanted Clint to meet him at the gazebo, at something-thirty."

"Or it could be a husband trying to arrange a romantic rendezvous for his wife last month, or a pair of fishermen wanting to get an early start on the day's catch this past summer," he said, suddenly dejected. "It's nothing much more than what you found, is it?"

"As much as we might like to, we can't manufacture evidence, Alex," she said. "Put your note with everything else. We can throw it all out when we get back home."

"I like the sound of that. Home. It sounds especially good when you say it. I'm sorry about our honeymoon. It's turned into a bit of a bust, hasn't it?"

Elise grabbed him and kissed him thoroughly. After she pulled away, she said, "Don't you dare apologize to me. I've been with you, and that's all I ever wanted. Everything else is just icing on the cake."

"That's one of the things I love about you, Elise. You're a woman with a very low bar."

She laughed. "You'd be surprised. Now let's get out of here before someone finds us snooping around."

"Okay. Let me check the hallway first." Alex poked his head out the door, and no one was in sight. "It's all clear," he said, and they both slipped out.

Elise locked the door behind them, and then she asked him, "What are we going to do with this key?"

"I have an idea," he said as he walked down to room number two, where the cart had been stored temporarily. Getting down on his hands and knees, he started to slide the key under the door when Elise put a hand on his shoulder.

"Stop," she said, and he immediately did as he was told. "What's wrong?"

"I hate to butt in, but wouldn't it be more convincing to unlock the door, put the key back where you found it, and then flip the lock before you close it again? I noticed you could do that with our room, so I have no reason to suspect that it won't work here as well."

Alex stood up, dusted off his hands, and looked at her sheepishly. "At least we know who the brains of the operation is," he said as he did as she suggested.

Elise smiled at him as he opened the door, returned the key, set the lock, and then closed it behind him. "We're both the brains."

"If you say so," Alex said just as he saw the door to another room start to open. That had been close!

It was the Eastons, and what was more, they weren't empty-handed. Each of them had suitcases and travel bags as well. Clearly they were leaving the lodge, whether it was good for Alex and Elise's investigation or not.

To Alex's surprise, the moment he saw them lurking in the hallway, Carlton turned to his wife and said, "See? Now do you believe me? I told you they were snooping on us!"

"What are you talking about?" Alex asked, shocked by the accusation.

"First we visit a nice little bed and breakfast in town, and who do we see as we're leaving? You two. Then we drive back here after checking out another place, and there you are again, right on our heels. It's like you're not even trying to be discreet. What do you want with us?"

"It was all just one big coincidence," Alex said.

"You're going to have to do better than that," Carlton said, clearly not believing him.

"It's true, though. Are you really leaving?" Elise asked them as she gestured to their bags.

"This place has been nothing but bad news for us," Val said. "It wasn't great before that man killed himself, but since he's been dead, we hear all kind of weird things at night. It's like there is some kind of haze over everything. Don't you see it?"

Alex looked around, but he didn't notice anything different about the space. "I'm not sure," he said.

"Well, it's there, trust me. We never even saw the man who committed suicide! Why would someone kill themselves in a room they weren't even staying in? It's downright creepy, if you ask me, and we're getting out of here."

"And it's going to rain more, too," Carlton added lamely.

"It's too late to use that excuse for our cover story, you idiot," Val told her husband. "You already told them the truth. Not that we need to lie to anyone. We're going, and that's that."

"Okay," Alex said. "Good-bye."

Val looked as though she'd been expecting him to put up a fight, so, with the wind out of her sails, at least temporarily, she turned to her husband and said, "Come on. I won't spend another second in this place I don't have to."

"I'm coming, enough with the scolding," Carlton said with an edge in his voice.

Once they were gone, Elise said, "So, that explains their odd behavior earlier. Can you imagine it? They were paranoid about us. I'd love to know what they would think if they knew some of the things we suspected them of."

"Elise, I didn't get the feeling that was two people fleeing the scene of the crime, did you?"

"No, it was more like two people who had enough and were getting out, no matter what."

"Maybe they don't need to be on our list anymore," Alex suggested.

"Maybe. Let's go join the others and see what's going on."

"I'm right behind you."

Alex and Elise went downstairs a few minutes later, and when they got there, they heard the Eastons telling Charlie the real story behind their sudden departure. The storm alibi hadn't been needed for anyone after all.

"Come on, folks, there's no reason to overreact. I'm sure I can make it worth your while if you just stay. How about a reduction in your nightly rate? I can make it very appealing for you to stay."

"Sorry, but it's not happening. Send us our final bill. Our accountant will pay it, but we're leaving."

They all watched the couple leave, and Alex turned to Charlie and put a hand on his shoulder. "Sorry about that. I know it's not easy." Alex had experienced his share of guests suddenly walking out on him, and he knew it wasn't an easy thing to handle. As an innkeeper, he couldn't help but feel responsible, no matter how erratic the guests' behavior might be.

"If this keeps up, I'm going under, and it's going to be sooner rather than later," Charlie mumbled to himself. "What else can go wrong?"

"I've learned never to ask that question, at least not out loud," Alex said, trying his best to cheer the man up.

Unfortunately, he failed miserably.

Chapter 14

"Do you mind if I join you again tonight?" Helen asked them after Alex and Elise took up their old, familiar table. "I know it's your honeymoon and all, but I'm getting really tired of eating alone. I don't have much more time here, but it's been dragging like chains around my neck waiting to be free."

"It must be hard on you," Alex told Helen as Zinnia took their drink orders. The waitress/maid looked as though she wanted to say something to Elise, but she must have changed her mind. Had she noticed the missing master key after all? Thank goodness they'd put it back on the cart. If she came out and asked them about it, Alex was going to suggest that she check again to be sure that it was missing, just to be on the safe side.

"It is. Especially these last few days."

"Because you were related to Clint somehow?" Alex asked, carefully watching for a reaction from the older woman.

It turned out that he hadn't had to watch all that carefully. "How could you? I can't believe you'd be heartless enough to say something like that to me!" Helen threw her napkin down and raced out of the room. Zinnia tried to stop her, but she wouldn't be deterred, so the waitress/maid ended up trailing behind her all the way up the stairs.

"What just happened?" Charlie asked as he rushed into the room. "Helen looked as though she just saw a ghost."

"I don't know what I said," Alex explained. "I just asked her if she was related to Clint, and she freaked out on me."

"Of course they were related! Everybody in town knows that, it's not exactly a state secret. She was his godmother. Is it any wonder she's a wreck?"

"Why does she stay here then? How can she manage to do it?" Elise asked, looking unhappily after the older woman.

"She doesn't have a choice. It's that whole ultimatum

thing she told you about before. That's what we were doing this morning, trying to talk the board out of making her stay for the full term, given what happened to Clint. The blackhearts refused to budge, even after they knew the circumstances. I have a feeling that when Helen returns from exile, heads are going to roll."

Zinnia rejoined them. "Nice move, Alex. Why didn't you punch her in the face while you were at it?"

"I'm sorry. I didn't know," Alex said lamely.

"His intentions were good," Elise tried to explain, but Zinnia wasn't having it.

"You know what, boss? You can wait on everybody tonight. I need a break."

"Come on, Zinnia. Don't be that way," Charlie said.

"What way is that?" she asked as she walked out of the dining room without even looking back. "If anyone needs me, I'll be with Helen."

"Again, I'm really sorry," Alex repeated to Charlie after Zinnia was gone.

"I'm the one who should be apologizing. You didn't know about Helen's bond with Clint. She practically raised that boy herself. It's a wonder she can stand being here at all," Charlie explained.

"So, that's why she was crying this morning after her hike," Elise said.

"She puts on a brave face," Charlie explained, "like she did when you both met her, but she's hurting deep inside."

"And I made it worse," Alex said, standing.

"Where are you going?" Charlie asked.

"To start apologizing," he replied.

"To anyone in particular?" Elise asked him as she stood as well.

"There's not any real order, but I seem to have made a general mess of things, so I'll start with whoever I find first."

"Dear, sweet, Alex," Elise said.

"You probably shouldn't go with me, Elise. I hate it that

I'm going to have to grovel. Doing it in front of you is just going to be that much harder."

"I understand, but that wasn't why I was standing. While you're doing that, I'm going to be tonight's server and wait on everyone else."

"Sit down, Elise. Alex, you, too," Charlie said in a commanding voice.

They had no choice but to follow his wishes. After they were seated again, the innkeeper said, "I've done just about everything possible to ruin your honeymoon, but this is where I draw the line, do you understand me? You're going to have a nice time, and it begins right now!"

Alex looked around the room, pretending to search for something.

"What are you looking for?" Charlie asked him.

"The brass band. A declaration that strong should at least be followed by a parade, don't you think?"

He wasn't sure if he'd taken the right tack with the innkeeper at first, but after a moment, Charlie joined him in his grin. "Okay, maybe I got a little carried away, but I meant what I said."

"A little?" Alex asked, not even trying to hide his laughter any more.

"A lot, then. I'm perfectly capable of stepping in when I'm needed. After all, this place is mine, at least for the moment." Charlie looked sad for a moment, but then he forced his smile to return. "Enough doom and gloom. Let me grab your drinks, and then I'll take care of our last remaining guests."

Alex glanced over and saw that, though they were still sitting at different tables, Erica and Ian were both watching everything closely. In all the fuss, he'd nearly forgotten that they were even still there.

"If you're sure," Alex and Elise said in nearly perfect unison.

"I'm positive," Charlie said.

The food was incredible as usual, but Alex had hoped that Carrie would come out of the kitchen after their last encounter. Though they'd appeared to patch things up with the chef, Alex wanted to make sure that things were still good between them. Instead, the lodge owner himself delivered the food, bussed the tables, and even refilled their drinks.

When it was time for dessert, Alex looked up to see Ian leave the dining room. Erica had been watching him the entire time, though discreetly, and the moment he was gone, she raced over to his table and snatched up his cell phone! Evidently he'd left it behind, and she wasn't going to let the opportunity to snoop get past her.

"Should you really be doing that?" he asked her from across the room.

"Why don't you kindly mind your own business," Erica said with a grin. "He's been making notes on this thing since he got here, and I'm going to find out what he's really been up to." Erica started playing with the display, and then she smiled brightly. "Can you believe it? He left it unlocked. Just because he can't get a signal doesn't mean that he can afford to be that sloppy." She started reading whatever was on the screen, and Alex and Elise watched as her expression started to darken exponentially as each second passed.

Ian must have soon realized his mistake, because he came back into the dining room, obviously missing his phone.

"Seriously? You're a spy?" she yelled at him, bringing Charlie and Carrie out of the kitchen to see what was going on.

"You had no right to look at my phone," Ian said as he tried to grab it. "Give it back to me."

"My parents pay you to follow me around! I own you right now. You're in no position to demand anything from me."

Ian finally succeeded in plucking it out of her hands. "Erica, it's not like that."

"Tell me then, what is it like?" Alex couldn't believe how the normally sweet Erica had turned into a screaming shrew.

"They're worried about you," Ian said, somehow managing to stay calm under the assault.

"What's going on?" Charlie asked as he approached the pair.

"Apparently my parents don't think I'm able to handle myself, so they hired a watchdog to look out for me," she explained.

"Is that true?" Charlie asked him.

Ian shook his head. "I'm not here looking out for her."

"That's a lie!" Erica shouted. "I saw your phone. You work for my parents, so don't try to deny it."

"I wasn't going to, but I'm not here to watch you. I'm supposed to keep Brad from getting in touch with you again. If he shows up, I'm supposed to politely ask him to leave, and if that doesn't work, I've been authorized to not be so delicate about making my request."

"Brad? What does he have to do with anything?" Erica asked. She was starting to calm down a little. "That's over."

"For you, perhaps," Ian said, "but he told your parents when you broke up with him that he would win you back, at any cost, whether you wanted him or not. It was a viable threat, Erica. After all, you're a desirable young woman."

"Don't try to change the subject. Besides, when Alex and Elise got here and it was suggested that we were a couple, you couldn't wait to deny the fact." She looked triumphant making the statement.

Ian just frowned. "That's only because I'm working, and I'm not supposed to get too close to you. The fact that I've been developing feelings for you is making things that much harder."

Erica looked as though she'd just been slapped. "What did you just say?"

"Don't make me repeat it," Ian said softly, for the first time showing a crack in his armor.

"I don't believe you," she said suddenly, but Alex had a hunch that she did. Not only that, but he had to wonder if she had feelings for him as well. Why else would she have reacted so strongly when she'd learned his secret? Erica stood up and started for the door.

"Where are you going?" Ian asked.

"I'm leaving," she said simply.

Everyone else followed as Ian trailed after Erica.

"What about your luggage?" Charlie asked as he saw her heading for the front door. "There's no reason to overreact."

"I'm not overreacting. Let my bodyguard bring my bags," she snapped.

"I'm not your bellboy," Ian said. "Could you hold still for one second and listen to reason?"

"I could, but I'm not going to." Clearly she had a full head of steam, and no one was going to stop her. Erica jumped into her car, with Ian close on her tail.

"Wow, who knew that we'd be getting dinner and a show?" Alex asked with a wry smile.

"Alex, do you honestly think this is funny?" Carrie asked him.

"No," he said. "Listen, I'm sorry about before. I thought we were good."

"We are, but that still doesn't mean that you should make light of the situation," she said. "I'd better get back into the kitchen."

Once Alex and Elise were seated again, they looked around and realized that they were the only ones still there. Zinnia was upstairs with Helen, Carrie was now in the kitchen, and Charlie had gone in to talk, and perhaps to lend a hand.

"We sure know how to clean out an inn," Alex said as he looked around.

"Practically none of this was our fault, though," she replied.

"I'm sorry about Helen. What do you think about Erica and Ian?" Alex asked.

"I suspected there was something going on there," she admitted.

"Seriously? I didn't have a clue. You knew he'd been

hired to watch her?"

"No, of course not," Elise said. "I'm talking about them having feelings for each other. I've seen too many sidelong looks pass between them to believe otherwise. The only problem is that all of our suspects are leaving the lodge. Alex, I'm afraid we're not going to be able to solve this murder at all."

"Maybe we should follow everyone else's lead and take off ourselves," Alex suggested.

"I'm not quite ready to give up yet, are you?" she asked.

"I'll do whatever you want to do," Alex said.

"You know what? Suddenly I don't feel like dessert. Do you want to take a walk with me?"

"You don't have to ask twice," Alex said as they stood up. "Just let me duck into the kitchen to tell Charlie what we're going to do."

"I'll come with you," Elise offered.

They walked in back and found Charlie doing his best to talk Carrie into staying. "I need you," he said.

"I'm sorry. I just can't do it anymore," she said as she began gathering her knives together. Alex knew she was serious. They'd had a chef stay with them at the inn, and he even took his knives with him on vacation. They were that important to him.

"At least give me a week to find your replacement," Charlie begged.

Carrie seemed to waver. "I don't know."

"I'll double your salary," he added desperately.

"Let me go home to my mother and sleep on it."

"That's all I ask," he said.

Carrie slipped past Alex and Elise with barely a nod, and then she was gone.

"That's it," Charlie said. "I'm officially finished. I can't run a lodge without a chef, or any guests, for that matter. The Bear Creek Lodge is going out of business."

"I'm sorry," Alex said as he patted the man on the shoulder. "Don't make any rash decisions just yet. You've got a great setup here. Luck just hasn't been going your way lately."

"Lately? How about since I first opened?" Charlie asked.

"Take a week and think about it," Elise said. "Things might seem brighter in the morning. If not then, perhaps in a few days. Look at it this way. What could it hurt?"

"I suppose I can only be so broke," he said with a shrug. "Care for some carrot cake? It's out of this world."

"Do you mind if we take a rain check?" Alex asked him.

"I get it. You're leaving, too, aren't you?" he asked with a layer of resignation in his voice that tore up Alex's soul.

"We just want to take a walk," Elise corrected him. "You're free to join us, if you'd like."

Alex wasn't sure inviting the morose innkeeper with them was the best idea, but Charlie declined anyway. "I've got to do dishes anyway." He shrugged as he looked at them in turn. "Don't offer to help."

"We won't," Alex said. He knew from firsthand experience that washing dishes could be therapeutic. Maybe it would give Charlie a chance to figure out what he was going to do next. Even if he didn't though, there was a comforting feeling in taking dirty dishes and making them clean again, like starting over fresh.

"We should grab our jackets," Alex said as they left the dining room. "The temperature's bound to be dropping."

"Okay," she agreed.

Once they were at the top of the stairs, Alex glanced over at Helen's room. "Elise, would it be okay if I tried to apologize now?"

"You should try," she said, patting his shoulder for encouragement.

Alex tapped on the door, and Zinnia opened it. He'd been expecting a blast from her, but instead, the maid/waitress just smiled. "You just saved me a trip."

"Listen, I just want to..."

She cut him off. "Save it, Alex. I'm sorry. I overreacted. You didn't do anything wrong."

"I'm sorry, too," Helen said from inside the room. "For goodness sake, Zinnia, let them in."

Alex and Elise joined her and were surprised to find that she was packing. "Are you leaving, too? I thought you had to stay," Elise said.

"I don't care," Helen said happily. "I'll take the anger management classes. The truth is, they might do me some good, but I can't spend another night here." She said the last bit as she glanced across the hall where her godson had been murdered.

"I'm driving her into town," Zinnia said. "How are things going downstairs?"

"Actually, it's kind of quiet now," Alex said.

"Really? We heard shouting earlier," Helen said.

"Oh. Erica found out that her parents had paid Ian to protect her from an ardent suitor. Ian confessed that he had feelings for her, and she stormed out."

"She's in denial. It was plain to see the way he felt," Helen said.

"Really? I didn't notice anything," Zinnia said.

"That's because you had your own drama to play out. Just tell him how you feel, child," Helen said.

"He'll just say that he's too old for me," Zinnia answered with a frown.

"Convince him otherwise," Helen said. She looked at her accumulated luggage and threw up her hands. "I'm packing an overnight bag. I'll have someone come out and get the rest of it another time. Are you ready?"

"I am if you are," Zinnia said.

"We'll walk you out," Alex offered.

"I'll be fine. You two enjoy your honeymoon. If you do it right, you'll only get one, and I'm sure the two of you are going to do it spectacularly."

"Thanks," they both said.

After the women left, Alex and Elise grabbed their jackets and headed outside.

"And then there were two," Elise said a little grimly.

"I'm starting to think maybe we should take off, too," Alex answered.

"You might be right. Let's take a walk and talk about it."

"I'm just not sure that I feel good about leaving Charlie alone out here," Alex said with a frown.

"Zinnia will be back as soon as she drops Helen off in town. Maybe the two of them need a little privacy to work things out."

He grinned at his wife. "Are you matchmaking, Elise?"

She shrugged. "Sometimes all people need is a little proximity and a chance to talk in peace and quiet."

As they walked out the back door and headed for the gazebo, Alex said, "There should be plenty of quiet for them both, then."

The gazebo had a lighting system around it, and as it began to get dark, the entire structure was illuminated. It was going to look awesome if Charlie could ever get someone to finish painting it. As they approached the structure, Alex saw something glimmering in the grass, and as he got closer, he saw that it was a beer bottle cap. Out of habit, he reached down and picked it up, but there were no trashcans in sight, so he shoved it into his pocket, along with a few cellophane wrappers and a fast-food napkin with the shop's brand embossed on the face of it. "It's beautiful out here, isn't it?" he asked her.

"Yes, but it will be getting dark in a few minutes." Elise took in the scenery, and then she said, "I'm afraid this trip is over, Alex. Tell you what. On our one-year anniversary, let's go someplace else."

"That sounds like a plan to me. Any ideas where you'd like to go?"

She shivered a little as the breeze kicked up, and it began to rain lightly again. "Someplace warm, maybe? How about a sandy beach."

"It's a date," he said.

She kissed him quickly, and then she said, "Let's go. I'm with Helen. I don't want to spend another night here, either."

As they headed back to the lodge, Alex heard something in the nearby woods. Was someone out there? Most likely it was just a squirrel or a bird, but he couldn't shake the feeling that they were being watched. Bear Creek Lodge was really starting to get to him, and he was glad that Elise had suggested they leave the place behind forever and head back to the comfort of Hatteras West.

Chapter 15

"I'm glad you're back. I was just about to come looking for you," Charlie said.

Alex saw Helen and Zinnia standing there with the innkeeper. "I thought you two were leaving?"

"The bridge didn't look safe, so we wanted Charlie to take a look," Zinnia said.

"We're coming with you," Elise said.

"Can we take your truck? My car is stuck in the mud in back," Charlie said.

"Let's go," Alex said.

"We'll follow you," Zinnia said.

They all headed back out into the rain. It was full-on dark now, and Alex crept along, worried about the dangerous drive. Charlie tried to start a few conversations, but Alex was focusing every bit of his energy on the road and on not killing them. He noticed that Elise sat between them, her hands gripped tightly to her thighs. She was scared too, with good reason, as far as Alex was concerned. It seemed to take forever to traverse the road, but they finally made it. Water was now lapping all around them, and Alex thought it had been extremely prudent of Zinnia to turn back.

"I want to get a better look," Charlie said as he got out into the storm.

"I'm going with him," Alex said as he reached under the seat for his heavy-duty flashlight.

"Me, too," Elise said. When Alex cocked one eyebrow at her, she grinned as she added, "For better or for worse, right?"

"Right," Alex said, proud to have her by his side.

The rain had turned icy, and Alex wondered if it might not turn to snow before daybreak, but that wasn't the immediate problem. The water was not just overlapping the sides of the bridge. It was having an impact on its structural integrity.

"It doesn't look good, does it?" Charlie asked.

"I wouldn't risk crossing it," Alex said, just as they heard the sound of metal straining against the current. It sounded as though the bridge itself was dying, and as they watched, it broke free and swept downstream. What had been a sedate little stream upon their arrival was now a seething torrent, destroying anything and everything in its path.

"We need to go back," Alex said as they watched the bridge submerge itself as it was pushed downstream.

"I know. I can't believe this," Charlie said as he turned back to the truck. "I'll go tell the ladies what's happening."

Alex swept his flashlight beam across the road before he and Elise went back to the truck, and his light caught a reflection in the woods. "Elise, what does that look like to you?"

"It's a police cruiser," she said. "But where's the cop who drove it there?"

Alex played the beam back and forth, but if there was anyone on the other side, he couldn't see him. "Hello? Is anyone there?" he shouted, but his words were drowned out by the rushing water and the pouring rain. "It's no use. Let's get back inside the truck."

She joined him, and a moment later, Charlie said, "Zinnia's not comfortable driving back, so I'm going to take her car. Are you all okay with that? There's a spot to turn around a few yards back. Give me a second, and then you can go. See you back at the lodge."

Once Charlie was gone, it was just the two of them.

"You didn't tell him about the police car," Elise said.

"Neither did you," he answered with a grin. "At this point, I'm not sure it would help matters. Maybe it got stuck, and someone came along and gave the officer a ride."

"Maybe," Elise said.

"Either way, there's nothing we can do about it now. How are we ever going to get out of here, Elise?"

"Somebody will wonder about us, and we know there are supplies in the kitchen, so we won't starve." She leaned into him as they waited for Charlie to turn around so they could make the same maneuver. "It's going to be fine."

"If I have you by my side, everything else is just a bonus," he said.

"Alex Winston, you say the sweetest things."

He chuckled a little despite their dire situation. "I don't say anything I don't mean." Alex noticed that Charlie had completed his maneuver and was now heading back to the lodge. He followed suit, and soon enough, they were all back, safe and sound, though a little wet from their impromptu trip.

"What do we do now?" Zinnia asked.

"I'm not going back up to that room," Helen said resolutely. "If I have to, I'll sleep on one of the couches."

"There's no need. I can make up Carrie's bed for you," Zinnia offered. "I'm afraid it's not luxury accommodations, though."

"I'll take it, and gladly," Helen said. "Could we have a fire first, though? I need to get the chill out of my bones."

"That's a good idea," Charlie said as he lit the fire in the hearth. "Let's all meet back here in a few minutes."

"I can make us coffee," Elise offered.

"Sold," Helen said.

Alex and Elise made their way back upstairs, quickly changed clothes, and then headed back down into the kitchen. Elise had a pot of coffee brewing, and after searching the cabinets, she pulled out a glass Mason jar. After opening the lid and smelling it, she grinned at Alex. "It's hot chocolate! Should I make some, too?"

"Why not? We can even have s'mores a little later," he said, doing his best to make the situation a happy one.

"If we have the supplies on hand, why not?"

If the lodge had marshmallows though, Alex and Elise couldn't find them. They did see some wedges of carrot cake, though, and on a hunch, they brought out enough for everyone as well. When they got back into the lobby, they found that the others were already there. Helen was sitting on the couch with a blanket wrapped around her shoulders, Charlie was tending the fire, and Zinnia was watching him with obvious emotions from a side chair.

After the five of them got their drinks of choice, Alex stared at the fire, wondering how this murder investigation had gotten away from him so completely. He hated feeling like a failure, but there was nothing he could do about it. All of his real suspects were gone, or worse yet, had never even been there at the lodge to begin with. He took little consolation in the fact that he and Elise had stumbled across it after the fact. When it came to his achievements, Alex always expected nothing but the best from himself. It was a high bar that was often difficult to meet, but that never stopped him from trying.

"I don't really feel like cake," Helen said. "Were there any other treats in the kitchen?"

"What did you have in mind?" Zinnia asked. "I'm sure I could round something up for you."

"My sweet tooth is aching for some sugar. I don't suppose there's any kids' candy back there, is there?"

"We have some Halloween candy left over in the pantry," she volunteered. "Let me go see what we've got."

As Alex stared at the flames, he let his mind roam a little. He hadn't even been paying all that close attention to the conversation, but then, it suddenly hit him.

He knew who the murderer was, and what was more, he thought he had a good chance of proving it!

Chapter 16

"Chief Laughlin killed Clint," Alex announced as soon as Zinnia returned.

"What are you talking about, Alex? It was a suicide," Helen said. "Must you keep opening up old wounds?"

"Helen, nobody in town believes that Clint killed himself. Why are you so ready to accept it?" he asked her.

"Because I rejected him. It was for his own good," she said, crying softly.

Zinnia put her arm around the woman. "You don't owe anyone an explanation," she said softly.

"I have to tell someone," Helen protested. "Clint needed money for one of his get-rich-quick schemes, but I drew the line. I told him he was going to have to stand on his own two feet and that I had to be tough with him. He yelled at me, even accused me of withholding my money out of spite because of his behavior towards the girls he dated. We had angry words, and the next thing I knew, he was dead by his own hand! What else could I think? Why would the chief kill him?"

"Because of Chloe," Alex said. He hadn't had a chance to discuss any of what he was saying and thinking with Elise, but there was no going back now. "Zinnia, you told us upstairs that Clint had taken advantage of the chief's daughter."

"It's true enough," Zinnia admitted. "Helen, I'm sorry. I know you loved your godson."

"I did, but that didn't blind me to what he did or the way he was," she said softly. "I accepted him the way he was."

"The chief wasn't so forgiving," Alex said. "You should have seen the way he defended her to Sandy in town. That's part of what gave him away."

"What was the other part?" Charlie asked.

"Candy wrappers," Alex said. "You're probably not going

to like the next part, and I'd like to apologize, but Elise and I felt as though we had no choice. We searched number seven without your permission."

"How did you get in?" Charlie asked, staring at Zinnia.

"I lifted a spare master key from her cart. It wasn't her fault," Alex explained.

"I thought it was missing. I'm glad you said something, because I thought I was losing my mind. When I checked the cart though, there it was."

"We put it back when we were through," Elise said. "I'm sorry, too."

"It's okay," Zinnia said. "Did you find anything?"

"We thought we found a partial note that might have been significant, but I'm beginning to believe that it wasn't important at all. What we did find were a few candy wrappers, along with some other things like buttons and paperclips."

"Hey, I never claimed to be a great maid," Zinnia said a little defensively. "And besides, I didn't have time to clean the room after the police released it. We're kind of shorthanded around here, in case nobody noticed."

"I'm glad you didn't get around to it," Alex said. "We never would have found the real clue if you had."

"I hate to burst your bubble," Charlie said, "but the chief came to examine the scene. He could have dropped the wrappers then by accident."

"Maybe, but that doesn't explain why I found the same type of cellophane at the gazebo, too."

"What ties that to the chief, though?" Helen asked.

"When he was arguing with Sandy about nosing into the murder, he reached into his pocket and pulled out a handkerchief. When he did, some of the same candy fell out of his pocket as well. He did it. I'd stake my life on it."

"Funny, but that's exactly what you've just done," the chief himself said as he walked down the steps and into the lobby.

His gun was out, and what was worse, it was pointed straight at Alex's heart.

"Why are you even here?" Alex asked him, wondering how he had managed to miss the man's presence at the inn.

"I've been looking for my truck keys since I dosed that sports drink with rat poison," the chief admitted. "You found them, didn't you?"

Charlie was about to speak up, but Alex knew if he let the innkeeper talk, they would all be dead.

"They're at the gazebo," Alex said. "You must have dropped them when you argued with Clint about your daughter. Is that when you swapped bottles on him?"

"He didn't even notice what I was doing," the chief said. "I confronted him about what he'd done to Chloe, and he didn't even bother denying it. He laughed at me! I wanted to strangle him on the spot, but a couple came along and spotted us talking. I asked around later and found out they were the Eastons. Where are they, by the way? I know the second floor is deserted, but they can identify me, too."

"They've left the lodge," Alex said, happy to be able to tell the truth.

"Okay, that's another loose end I'll have to take care of later if it becomes a problem for me."

"Why did you take him upstairs?" Elise asked. "That was an awfully big risk, wasn't it?" As she asked the question, Alex began looking around for a weapon. The iron poker was too far away, and the lamp closest to him was too flimsy to do much damage. Was there nothing he could use to defend them?

As he kept searching for some kind of weapon, the chief replied to Elise's question. "I had to get him out of sight, and I knew he took his naps upstairs," he said. "I convinced him that if he'd write out an apology to Chloe, I'd leave him alone forever. The fool actually believed me. He started to write something once we got there, and I told him I was thirsty as I pretended to reach for his bottle. That's when he grabbed it instead and took a healthy swallow, which I figured he would do just to spite me. It was amazing how quick that stuff worked! Anyway, I got out of there, and luck was with me. I had a cover story all ready if anyone saw me, but I got away clean."

"Except for your keys," Alex said.

"Yeah, except for those. Anyway, I've been coming back when I had the chance ever since, trying to find them so no one would connect me with what happened. I would have been able to sell the suicide story if you hadn't stuck your noses into it. I'm not going to mind killing you at all," he said.

"But not before you get your keys," Alex reminded him. If he could get him outside, maybe he'd have a chance of overpowering the cop. Laughlin was older and overweight. If Alex could get a clear line on him, he might just have a fighting chance.

Even if he didn't make it, it would be better than allowing them all to be executed, gangster style.

"Let's go, then," the chief said. Alex started to stand when the police chief added, "All of you."

"You don't need them," Alex protested.

"I'm not leaving a soul here alone. Now move it!"

Helen looked almost comatose, and Alex was worried about her state of mind.

It turned out that he shouldn't have.

As Helen trudged past the police chief, she launched herself onto him.

It was the bravest, and possibly the dumbest, thing that Alex had ever witnessed, but he didn't stand around admiring her.

He leapt for the hand holding the gun.

As they fought for control, it went off, sending a bullet screaming into the rafters. It was a good thing no one was upstairs after all. From the look of things, it went straight into one of the guestrooms on the second floor.

Elise joined him an instant later, and Charlie and Zinnia weren't far behind. They collapsed on the man like a bucket of bricks, and he went down in the hail of bodies. Alex forced the gun out of his hand, and then he ordered the rest of them to get up.

Helen got in a fierce kick to the cop's ribs after she stood, but Alex didn't blame her a bit, not after what he'd done to her godson.

"Do you have any rope?" Alex asked, panting from the effort.

"Yeah, it's in the storage room," Charlie volunteered.

"I'll get it," Zinnia offered.

"You have his truck keys, don't you?" Alex asked the innkeeper.

"They're in the lost and found under the desk," he explained as he retrieved them.

The chief looked outraged. "They were here all along? You lied to me!"

"So sue me," Alex said.

Zinnia came back with a stout rope and started to hand it to Charlie.

"I'll take that," Helen said.

"Can you tie a knot he can't get out of?" Charlie asked her.

"Oh, he won't get away," she said with grim satisfaction.

As Helen began tying the chief's hands behind his back, he protested, "Hey, that's too tight."

Charlie leaned over, checked out the knot, and then said, "Maybe you should loosen it up a little."

"Not a chance," Helen said.

The chief responded by lashing out his legs, catching Charlie in the shin.

"There's more rope where that came from," Zinnia said. "Should I get it for his legs?"

"That's probably a good idea," Alex said, still holding the gun on the rotten chief of police.

"I'm done fighting," the chief said.

"Maybe so, but we're not taking any chances," Alex said.

Once he was secured, Alex put the gun away, though he kept it in his pocket, just in case he needed it. As Elise approached him, he said, "Sorry I didn't say anything to you first, but I just worked it all out."

"I'm fine with the way you handled things," she said.

"Don't kid yourself. If Helen hadn't distracted him, we'd probably all be dead right now."

"It took all of us," Helen said. Alex was afraid to let her get anywhere near the chief. He was afraid of what she might do and how much she'd regret it later. It was a heady thing, having vengeance before you like that, and if he could help Helen resist the temptation, he'd do his best.

"What do we do now?" Zinnia asked.

"What can we do?" Charlie asked. "There's no cell phone reception, the landline is inconsistent on its best days, and the bridge is washed out. We'll just have to wait for someone to notice that we're missing."

"I have to go to the bathroom," the chief said.

"Hold it," Helen replied savagely. "Or don't. I don't care one way or the other."

"It brings up a good point," Elise said. "How long do you think it will take, Charlie?"

"I have no idea," he said as they heard something approaching from the air.

"Is that a helicopter?" Zinnia asked.

"It must be," Alex said as it got closer and closer.

"Let's go see who it is," Charlie said.

"You all go ahead," Helen suggested. "I'll stay here with the chief."

"I'll stay, too," Alex quickly volunteered.

Helen looked extremely upset by his offer, but she didn't protest.

As they waited, Alex said, "I'm sorry about Clint."

"So am I, for a great many reasons," she replied.

"He deserved exactly what he got," the chief said.

Helen slapped his face, but Alex made no move to stop her. After he protested, she said, "One more word out of you and I'm going to take that gun and shoot you with it. Do you understand me? Don't talk. Just nod."

Chief Laughlin nodded.

It was a serious situation, but from the tension of it all, it was all that Alex could do not to smile.

Officer Ford came in and barely glanced at his former boss. "Where's his weapon?" he asked.

"It's right here," Alex said, pulling it from his pocket slow and easy.

"Good."

"How did you know the chief was here?" Alex asked as he handed over the weapon.

"I found his squad car parked on the road, so it wasn't tough to figure out where he was. He's been acting weird, even for him, since this whole thing happened with Clint, and I've had my own suspicions, so I asked a buddy to fly me over here in case you were in trouble. It was tight, but he managed to do it." He looked at his boss and added, "Looks like I didn't need to do that, though. You all took care of the situation." Turning back to Alex and Helen, he said, "You can go on out now. The chopper will get you out of here."

"What about him?" Helen asked.

"I'll be here with him until the chopper comes back," Ford replied. He nudged the chief with his foot. "What's wrong? Run out of things to say?"

The chief looked at Helen warily and then shook his head in silence. "He was given an incentive not to speak," Alex explained.

"One of these days you'll have to tell me about it. Now go on. Stan won't wait around for you forever."

Alex did as he was told, glancing back at the police chief one last time before he left Bear Creek Lodge forever. He wished Charlie the best of luck, but he'd had enough. It was time to get back to Hatteras West and find out what his life was going to be like with Elise, his new bride.

Chapter 17

A week later, they were back at Hatteras West and just getting used to running the inn as husband and wife. "We got a postcard from Zinnia," Elise said as she handed the mail to Alex. Though Alex loved the walk to the mail and back, he and Elise had been trading off days, since she enjoyed the stroll as well. They'd tried walking to collect the mail together at first, but since they spent virtually every waking second together, even the newlyweds could use a short respite from each other.

"What does it say?" he asked.

"She and Charlie are coming next week."

"Is he shutting the lodge down?" Alex asked.

"No, I don't think so. I think Zinnia's given him new hope," she said with a smile.

"Does that mean they're dating?" Alex asked.

"I don't think it's gone that far, but it can't be too long before they start, if you ask me." She put the rest of the mail on the front desk. "We have three guests coming this afternoon. It's good to be working again, isn't it?"

"I don't feel like we ever really stopped," Alex admitted.

"It wasn't much of a honeymoon, but I never needed a fancy trip to start off my marriage to you," she said as she put her arms around her husband.

"I couldn't agree with you more," Alex replied.

All was well and good with his world, but he knew that things couldn't stay that way forever. Something was bound to happen at the inn; it always did, but when it did occur, he'd be ready to tackle it, with Elise right by his side.

And that made him a very happy man indeed.

To learn more about Tim Myers's novels, please visit www.timmyersfiction.com.

Books by Tim Myers
Lighthouse Mystery Series
Innkeeping with Murder
Reservations for Murder
Murder Checks Inn
Room for Murder
Booked for Murder
Key to Murder
Ring for Murder
Candlemaking Series
At Wick's End
Snuffed Out
Death Waxed Over
A Flicker of Doubt
Waxing Moon
Soapmaking Series
Dead Men Don't Lye
A Pour Way to Dye
A Mold for Murder
Cardmaking Series
Invitation to Murder
Deadly Greetings
Murder and Salutations
Slow Cooker Mysteries
Slow Cooked Murder
Simmering Death
Standalone Cozy Mysteries
A Family of Strangers
Coventry
Volunteer for Murder
Paranormal Adult
Werewolf PI
Zombie PI
Romantic Fantasy
The Fairy Godfather
Suspense

Caved In
Cornered
Hunted
Iced
Trapped
Short Story Collections
A Touch of Romance
Beauty Times 3
Can You Guess What's Next? Vol. 1
Can You Guess What's Next? Vol. 2
Crimes with a Twist
Dark Shots
Dark Sips of Mystery
Did You Solve the Crime? Vol. 1
Did You Solve the Crime? Vol. 2
Did You Solve the Crime? Vol. 3
Hidden Messages
Long Shots
Marriage Can Be Murder
Money Mysteries
Murder Is a Special Occasion
Murder Nine to Five
Pet Mysteries
Repeat Performances
Senior Sleuths Again
Senior Sleuths Times 3
Turning the Tables
Middle-Grade Readers
Book of Time and Ben Franklin
Book of Time and Thomas Edison
Book of Time and Archimedes
Crispin Livingston Hughes, Boy Inventor
Emma's Emerald Mine
Lost in Monet's Garden
Lost in Picasso's Cubes
Young Adult Mysteries
Lightning Ridge

Rebuilding My Life
Tackling the Truth
Voltini
Young Adult Sci-Fi & Fantasy
Paranormal Kids
Paranormal Camp
Wizard's School Year 1: The Wizard's Secret
Wizard's School Year 2: The Killing Crystal
Books by Tim Myers writing as Chris Cavender
Pizza Mystery Series
A Slice of Murder
Thin Crust Killers
Pepperoni Pizza Can Be Murder
A Pizza to Die For
Rest in Pizza
Killer Crust
The Missing Dough
Books by Tim Myers writing as Casey Mayes
Mystery By The Numbers
A Deadly Row
A Killer Column
A Grid for Murder

Made in the USA
Monee, IL
02 March 2021